The trailer swung to the left, hitting Eric's old Ford and crushing the side in before hurling it down the embankment, crushed beyond recognition.

Eric knew nothing, saw nothing and did not feel the blood flooding into his ears. Only Jessie lay conscious, imprisoned by the smashed side of the Ford, smelling the blood coming from Eric, dazed, but already overcome by a desire to escape from the wreckage.

A Home For JESSIE

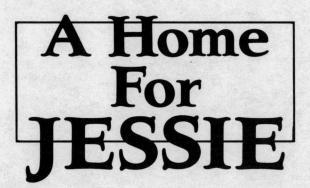

A Home For JESSIE

by Christine Pullein-Thompson
cover illustration by Doug Henry

Published in this edition in 1988 by
Willowisp Press, Inc.
401 East Wilson Bridge Road
Worthington, Ohio 43085

© Copyright Christine Pullein-Thompson 1986

Printed in the United States of America

10 9 8 7 6 5 4 3 2 1

ISBN 0-87406-335-3

One

"I'LL take her now," said the large man with old-fashioned braces holding up stained trousers, and a greasy cap on his head. "I'll drop her in the stream and let her drown: there's no other way, my dear."

The woman had grey hair too, thinning on top, and wore a sagging skirt, a blouse and husky jacket.

"Why not take her to the vet, Joe? Drowning isn't legal. You know that," she said.

"Because the vet will talk, Eileen. He'll tell his customers that Joe Clay's best bitch had a pup with white under its chin and two pink claws, and no one will want her pups any more," said the man, dropping a small bundle of black pup, its eyes not long open, into a hemp sack. "I don't like doing it, my dear, but there's no other way; because if anyone sees her and finds out the truth, Marlborough Melody's pups won't be worth a fivepenny piece."

He put the sack over his back. In her pen, Marlborough Melody was licking her five other pups, unconcerned. The evening sun shone out of a darkening sky. The man bent down to pick up a handful of stones. "She'll die quick. She won't know a thing," he said.

"She won't. Why not knock her on the head?" asked the woman.

But long ago the man had seen his dad drowning kittens, a whole litter in one sack held down in the rainwater tank. No one had bothered then. No one had said, "You can't do it. It isn't legal," and the kittens had soon died and been buried. He planned to bury the pup too. He would bring the sack back and bury her in the garden. That way no one need ever know she had existed.

He walked past pens of Labradors, some among the best in the land, but none better than Marlborough Melody. She had been champion at Cruft's, the greatest British Dog Show, and champion Labrador three years running at the Counties' Show. He had never owned such a bitch before, and then she had produced this pup with white on it. It had seemed impossible at the time. At first he had blamed the sire, but the sire was a champion too, with over a hundred pups to his name. And he could not risk his best bitch being suspect. It would make all her progeny the same, so that whenever a speck of white appeared on a black Labrador, people in the know would say, "Must be a throw back to Joe Clay's bitch." No reputable breeder could risk that. It would have been different if Marlborough Melody had been old, but this was only her third litter. She might well have another four or five litters, each worth more than a thousand pounds, perhaps as much as three thousand. It was far too much to risk for one pup.

"I'll bring her back and bury her here," he told his wife. "That way no one need know anything."

His wife turned away and went back into the small untidy kitchen, wiping tears from her eyes and thinking: we should have kept the pup, found her a home later, given her away. But it was no good arguing with Joe: she had learned that years ago, soon after they were married. He had to have his way—always. Her views carried no weight with him, never had, never would. The old Labrador which lived inside greeted her with wagging tail, but she did not see him, for all she could see now was the poor wee pup drowning in a weighted sack down in the stream where the water-cress grew.

Matt Painter was bored as he idly kicked a stone up and down the drive of the house his parents had rented for a year. He was small for his age, which was ten, going on eleven; dark-haired, brown-eyed, his face freckled round his small upturned nose. He had few friends, for his parents never stayed long enough in one place for him to make lasting relationships. He had never had time to put down roots, and seemed to be living on the surface of life. Because of this his greatest ambition was to have a job which kept him in one place, unlike his father's work which forced his father to spend most of his life abroad, moving from country to country, selling British goods, setting up exhibitions and new companies, always on the go.

Long ago Matt had decided he wanted to be a doctor or a veterinary surgeon, something which would keep him in the same place. Failing that, he would be a gardener, with his own small market garden. He had only two friends now, Anne and James. James was a lean lanky boy with no father and a mother so fat that she looked like a hippopotamus. No one besides Matt liked James, because he was the sort of person who always says the wrong thing at the wrong moment, and can never see a joke. Often James was the butt of the whole class, for somehow he never seemed in touch with what was going on.

Anne was different. "A real live wire," Matt's mother called her; full of laughter, blonde, tubby, bustling, always running when she could be walking. Good at games, useless at math, she made friends quickly and then discarded them, but not Matt. Matt was someone special.

Matt's mother worked part time in the local doctor's office. She was a trained secretary, quick and efficient, always able to find a job. Matt's father was efficient too. With dark moustache and hair already turning grey, he liked a place for everything and everything in its place.

Matt was not like either of them. Born under the sign of Virgo, on September 8, he was a lover of the earth, and would have liked a garden of his own. A small plot would have done, but because they were always moving this was impossible. All he could do was to water other people's plants, which was not the same as having his own. So that was why he was discontentedly kicking a stone along the long gravelled drive which belonged to someone else, until he decided to go down to the water meadows to see whether the primroses were out yet.

Joe Clay did not hurry. The evening sun was shining and the water meadows were damp beneath his laced-up shoes. As he walked, he remembered again his father drowning the kittens, litter after litter, sometimes three in a year. In the end the old mother cat had died, worn out by producing so many kittens.

Cows grazed the water meadows. They stopped to watch him pass and he could hear the pup whimpering in the sack, feel it moving, but there was no turning back now. It was only one pup after all, and what is one pup in a world like ours, he thought, as he felt in his pocket for his pipe, finding it there, knowing that it would give him solace afterwards.

Most of the stream was almost still and clogged with watercress, but he managed to find an open stretch where the water ran clear and deep. He opened the sack to put the stones from his pocket inside; and, seeing light, the pup whimpered hopefully and tried to suck his fingers. He tied a piece of cord round the top of the sack, cutting the ends with the penknife he always carried. Now the moment had come and, because he was basically a kind man, he tried to think of other things as he carefully lowered the sack into the stream before putting a stone on top and then hurrying away to sit on a stile behind the willow trees, smoking his pipe and intending to wait there until the pup had died.

Matt met Anne as he hurried toward the water meadows. She, like him, was destined to be forever moving on. Other children were always saying, "Oh, you are so lucky. You've been *everywhere*," but Anne knew that it was not like that. She had been to four different schools in twelve years, if you included play schools. She felt that she belonged nowhere and would have liked to be able to say, "I'm a Londoner," or "I come from Oxfordshire." Instead she could only say, "Dad's in the army. We move around. Next term I'm starting at a boarding school and I know I shall hate it, but . . ."

Matt was her best friend, but they were like people passing through a landscape together; soon they would both move on.

"Where are you off to?" she asked now, catching up with Matt.

"Dunno. Down to the stream, I suppose," he said.

She fell in beside him, her stride matching his. She was wearing jeans, orange socks, a thick sweater with a horse's head on it, and trainers.

"When I go to boarding school I shall be able to ride: there are stables attached. I may even be able to have my own pony," she said.

"Lucky you. I'm not going to boarding school when we move to the USA," Matt said. "Mum doesn't want me sent away to school."

"Because of her brother; the one who hated it so much he nearly killed himself? Your Uncle Eric?" Anne asked.

Matt nodded. "Not that I would do that. I'm not that much of a fool; but she reckons I would be unhappy, because I hate cricket and rules. I'm a bad mixer too."

"I shall hate it too; except for the riding of course, but Dad's going to Belize, and girls don't have much of a time there," said Anne. They climbed a stile and ran on.

The sack in the stream was hardly moving now. Joe Clay was laying down his pipe, thinking, another minute and I can go home. He was seeing himself digging a hole, his wife calling, "All over? Have you killed the pup?" the tone of her voice making him feel like a murderer.

And yet he had not wanted to kill it. It was simply that there was no other way and he had to make a living. People thought he was rich because his dogs were successful, but they never considered the vet's bills, the rates, the food so many dogs needed, the cost of traveling to shows where the prizes were hardly large enough to pay for the petrol. He knocked his pipe out on a stone and stood up slowly, swaying slightly.

"There's a sack in the stream. It wasn't there yesterday," Matt said.

"Just rubbish. People are always dumping rubbish," answered Anne. "They should be prosecuted, but they never are. It drives Mum mad. The other day she leapt from her car and shouted at someone throwing sweet papers out of a car window."

"It's got a stone on it. Look!" Matt said, bending over the stream where the water ran so clear that you could see your face in it.

"Be careful. It could be a bomb or something. Is it ticking?"

"A bomb in a stream?" Matt was pulling the sack out now. "Here, give me your knife," he said, for Anne always carried a tenpence, a penknife and string in her pocket. They often came in handy, and today was no exception.

Matt could feel his heart beating now. "It'll be kittens. People are always getting rid of kittens by drowning. It's terribly cruel. They should have their cats neutered. It's irresponsible not to," Anne told him, as she shut up her penknife. He put his hand in the sack and pulled out the pup and cradled it in his arms. "It's still breathing," he cried.

Anne pulled her sweater over her head and handed it to him. "Wrap it up. Quick," she said. "Hold it upside down so the water runs out. Quick, or it'll suffocate." Water poured from the pup's nose. Then they wrapped it in the sweater and started to run home, Anne crying, "How could anyone do it? How *could* they? They should be prosecuted." Matt thought that that was typical of Anne—she always wanted people prosecuted, while at this moment all he wanted was for the puppy to survive. Nothing else mattered. He did not care who had put it in the stream to drown. It was his now, because he had found it. Fate had sent it to him and no one was going to take it away, now or ever.

Joe Clay watched them go before walking down to the stream to pick up the sack, half-pleased and half-dismayed by what had happened.

As long as they don't go to the police, he thought. As long as they keep quiet. If they go to the police I shan't say anything. No one knows how many pups Marlborough Melody had this time. There's no evidence against me, so I'm all right. I shan't have to dig the hole either.

Two

THEY put the pup in a cardboard box with newspaper in it near the Aga cooker in the kitchen in Matt's house.

"We need a baby's bottle. I'll run home and get my little brother's," Anne said.

"Can you? I mean, won't someone mind?"

"They won't have to. He's got three. What baby needs three bottles, I ask you?" replied Anne, laughing.

They fed the pup together and Matt named her Jessie, because it would be easy to call. They wondered why she was being drowned but could not find the answer. Matt saw himself growing up with a black dog called Jessie shadowing him, but he knew it was only a fantasy because life was not like that. One day quite soon he would have to go and then Jessie would have to find a new home. Anne knew it too but was too wise to mention it. So they sat in the kitchen, watching the pup sleep, saying nothing.

When Matt's parents returned from work and shopping they were not pleased to see Jessie sleeping so comfortably by the Aga. Anne had gone home by this time, and Matt was making himself a cold drink.

"You know we can't keep a dog. I've told you so

time and time again, Matt. Are you thick or something?" his father asked.

"She was in a sack being drowned," Matt replied, looking at his town-suited father. "Did you want us to leave her there to die?"

"She's sweet," exclaimed his mother, kneeling down. "What breed is she? She's not a mongrel, that's for sure. Labrador or retriever, I should say. But she's got a patch of white under her chin."

"Which was why she was being drowned," said Matt's father. "She's a Labrador, and Labradors can't have any white on them, not if they are show animals—*and* she's got pink claws as well." Matt's father knew about dogs; he knew about everything come to that, or thought he did.

"You can't keep her, Matt. You know that, don't you?" his mother asked. "It wouldn't be fair on her; you must see that . . . Would Anne take her?"

"No, dogs give her Mum asthma; she doesn't like dogs. And *she's* moving too. All right?" Matt said.

"There's no need to snap." His father was opening letters now.

One day I shall be old enough to do what I want. One day I shall own my own dog, thought Matt. One day, but how many years lay between now and then!

"She can stay for a bit, but we must start looking for a home for her," his mother said. "We can't keep her because of quarantine regulations. You must see that, darling. If we took her to America, we couldn't bring her back."

"Yes, find a home right away before you get too attached, Matt. Do you hear me?" asked his father.

17

"Yes, Dad. But she may die. She's only tiny. She's still on a bottle."

"Ten days at the most. Right, Matt?"

Matt nodded miserably. "A week, ten days. That means by next Friday she must be gone. It's cruel to be kind, Matt. We can't take a dog abroad with us. There's too many laws and when we returned she would be in quarantine for six months or more, in solitary confinement, Matt. That's a terrible thing to inflict on a dog," his father said. "I'm not being mean. I'm thinking of the pup . . ."

Matt knew it was true. His Dad *was* thinking of the pup and he was right; he always was. But Matt felt sick just the same.

"Some kids found the pup, ran off with her, but maybe it was for the best," Joe Clay told his wife.

"As long as they don't go to the police," she said.

"Or guess where she came from and turn up here making a nuisance of themselves," he said.

"What sort of kids were they?"

"All right, I should say. A boy and a girl. I don't know them: they weren't locals, but all right, I should say."

Now it was nearly Friday. Jessie had grown and could lap now. She was chewing things. She had become more of a puppy, less of a round bundle, but she still had a baby smell and she still liked her bottle.

Anne and Matt were walking home together from school. "What are you going to do?" Anne was saying. "Will your father remember what he said?"

"My father never forgets anything. Mum says his brain is a computer . . ." Matt answered, walking slowly, his hands in his trousers pockets. "A computerized brain, that's what he's got . . ."

"You're not being very nice," Anne said.

"He knows everything. He never makes a mistake, never loses his train ticket, spills ink or drops a plate. And he's so tidy it's unbelievable, simply unbelievable. The top of every bottle must be screwed on just so. Even the butter has to be straight in the butter dish. And you know what *I'm* like . . ." finished Matt.

"We could hide Jessie, pretend she's gone," suggested Anne.

"But where?"

"In your tool shed."

"But she yaps now. Dad will hear her. They are only puppy yaps, but he hears everything."

"There must be something we can do!"

"I'll try to get them to give me another week. Just one more week I'll say."

"And then?"

"I don't know."

"But you haven't even *tried* to find Jessie a home. What about an advertisement in the local shop, or the paper?"

"I'll think about it."

"But you must do it, for Jessie's sake, don't you see?"

"Not yet. We may never go to America," said Matt

19

obstinately. "Something may happen. Dad may lose his job, Mum be taken ill. There's still six whole months left. There isn't any hurry. It's just that Dad's always in a hurry. He likes everything tied up, that's all. And she's so happy with us."

"But every day will make it one day harder," Anne insisted.

"I've never had an animal before, can't you understand?" cried Matt, running down the road, tears blinding him. "She's my first one . . ."

He picked Jessie up when he reached home and walked round the house singing to her. She recognized him now. She wagged her little tail when she saw him, and her eyes were beginning to lose their baby look. Then he said, "You're not going. Not now, not ever. I'm staying behind. They can go to America without me. I don't care, so that's that, Jess."

"Well?" asked his mother, arriving from work.

"Well?" repeated Matt, Jessie still in his arms.

"Have you found her a home?"

"Not yet."

"You know what your Dad said . . ."

Matt nodded. His throat was growing tight and tears pricked in his eyes. "I'm staying behind . . . I'm not going to America."

"Now I know you *are* mad," his mother said, changing her shoes. "We'll find you a pet in America. You can have a tortoise, or a cat; something easily disposed of when we leave."

"You mean 'put down'," shouted Matt.

"No, I don't. I mean, found a new home. You can't ruin all your chances for a little pup you picked up out

20

of a ditch."

"Out of a stream actually," Matt shouted.

"You heard what your Dad said. I'll put up an advertisement at work tomorrow morning. What shall I put? LABRADOR PUPPY FREE TO GOOD HOME. How's that?"

Matt could not think of an answer, so he went upstairs to his room slamming the door after him. He lay on his bed and let Jessie crawl over him. He kept seeing her growing up and himself somewhere else, and it was unbearable.

Later his father banged on the door and called, "I want to see you, Matt. Come out into the passage, please . . . Hurry up now, I'm a busy man. Don't keep me waiting: there's a good boy."

Matt left Jessie on his bed. Then, shutting the door after him, he stood in front of his father, a tear trickling down his cheek.

"Have you found Jessie a home? Tomorrow's Friday. You know what I said. Are you keeping your side of the bargain?"

"*I* never made a bargain, and I'm still looking . . ."

"Looking isn't good enough. I want one found, before the dog becomes established here. Soon she'll be piddling on the carpets and chewing up the chair legs. This isn't our house, Matt. Be reasonable," his father said.

"I am being reasonable."

"What have you done?"

"Nothing," replied Matt honestly. "But I'm *going* to . . ."

"Going to isn't good enough."

"I haven't had time," Matt said. "I'm at school. Remember?"

"There's no need to be rude. You can ask around at school. If you don't find a home by next weekend, she's going to the vet. Is that understood?"

Matt returned to his room, slamming the door after him. He curled up on his bed and told himself not to cry because he was supposed to be too big to cry. Perhaps James will have us to live with him, he thought. Mum and Dad can pay for us while they are in the USA, and I won't have to change schools. I can stay in England for another two years then.

The next day he spoke to James in break. "How about me and Jessie living with you next year?" he asked. "Then we wouldn't have to go abroad. My parents would pay your mum, of course," he added.

James looked away across the tarmac to the tall trees which lined the playing fields. "You've never been to our place, have you?" he asked.

"Not inside," Matt said.

"There's not a lot of room. You see, Mum has a friend living with us. He's called Steve and he's out of work most of the time and somehow I don't think you would get on. He would probably kick Jessie and then you would get upset. Anyway we live in a council house and you're not allowed to keep dogs in council houses."

Matt looked at James and knew he was speaking the truth. He didn't know what to say. "You don't know how lucky you are with your parents," James continued. "You really don't . . . You are *so* lucky . . . And think of going to America. I would give all I've

22

got to go. Jessie will be all right; she'll manage."

"But she won't be *mine* any more and I want something I can call my own . . ."

"So do I, but I can't have it," James said.

"I mustn't give in. I'll never give in. I found Jessie and finding is keeping. I'll even run away if I have to, you'll see . . ." Matt said.

Three days later when Matt had just returned from school the telephone rang. He picked it up, and a voice said, "I'm ringing about the Labrador puppy you've advertised. Have you still got her?"

"Which advertisement?" Matt asked to gain time.

"The one at the doctor's office."

"Can I have your name, please?" Matt asked, his heart pounding.

"I'm Mrs. Bennet from the sweet shop. I want her as a guard dog."

Matt saw Jessie chained, day and night. He saw her in a kennel without bedding. He saw her belonging to a plump old lady who did not care, who just wanted a guard dog.

"She's got a home," he said, putting down the receiver.

Jessie could give a paw now when asked, and could go to heel. She was always waiting for Matt when he returned from school.

Days passed, limpid sunny days. School ended for the summer. Another voice telephoned asking for Matt's mother. "It's about the puppy," the voice explained.

Matt's mother was in the kitchen and Matt shut the door before he said, "I'm sorry, she's got a home."

"Why don't you take down the advertisement then?" snapped the voice at the other end of the line, slamming down the receiver.

"Who was that?" called his mother.

"Wrong number," replied Matt, going to the window and looking at the garden without seeing it, feeling guilty because he had lied . . .

His father was becoming impatient now. He watched Matt playing with Jessie in the garden. "She's got to go. What happened to the advertisement you put up?" he asked his wife.

"There were no inquiries."

"The longer we wait, the harder it will be."

"I know. *I'm* fond of her too."

They sat in deckchairs watching Matt and he could feel their eyes boring into his back.

"If you don't find a home for that dog soon, she'll go to a home for stray dogs, because that's what she is, Matt—a stray," shouted his father. "I'm giving you one more week."

"Okay," Matt said. "I'll try, but it's got to be a *good* home." He and Jessie spent the rest of the evening with Anne. Matt felt safer there, even though Anne's mother did not like Jessie. They played Scrabble and Jessie lay at his feet, small and trusting, waiting for him to move and say the magic words, "Time to go home."

"The longer you keep her, the worse it will be for

both of you," Anne said.

And Matt knew it was true. "I keep hoping we won't go away after all, that something will happen to stop us, a war or something."

"You can't hope for a war just to save Jessie," Anne said.

"Well, Dad could break his leg."

"He would still go. A broken leg wouldn't stop your Dad: you know that," Anne answered.

Matt imagined his father hobbling onto an airliner on crutches. Anne was right—a broken leg would not stop him going. He wanted this new assignment in Florida. It was a plum job. Nothing would stop him going except death, and Matt did not want his father dead.

"I would go to boarding school if it would help," he said.

"You must stop being selfish. Think of Jessie before it's too late," Anne said, looking at him earnestly. "What's best for *her*?"

"Staying with me. She trusts me, believes in me. I can't just get rid of her, can't you see?" shouted Matt. "I *found* her . . ."

He took Jessie to the vet for vaccination against various diseases. A strange assortment of animals were waiting. The cost was eighteen pounds, and he had only five in his pocket. When he gave his name the receptionist said, "That's all right: we'll send the bill to your father . . ." and a cold shudder ran down his spine. "Bring her back in six weeks then, okay?" she added.

"Okay . . ."

It was a summer evening but it did not feel like summer. Earlier Jessie had chewed his mother's new shoes which had cost thirty pounds, and the veterinary surgeon's bill had come as well. "Matt," said his mother. "Why didn't you have the bill sent to me? Your father is absolutely furious. You know how he is."

"But she *had* to have them, and Dad's rich. I paid five pounds; it's all the money I had," Matt shouted.

"I wish you had never found her," his mother said. "I wish you had passed by without seeing the sack; really I do . . ."

"It's not *my* fault we are always travelling. I wish I had different parents, poor parents who loved dogs and had a shabby house and stayed in the same place for ever. I wouldn't care how poor they were. I wish you stayed at home and were there when I got home from school and made lovely cakes and things," shouted Matt. "I wish . . ."

"*I* wish we could keep Jessie, but we can't. We can't give up a job for a puppy, can't you see, Matt? Your father has been living for this opportunity for years. It's a tremendous step up and you will love Florida. I know you will; everyone does. The climate is fantastic."

"I don't care about the climate. I don't want to go," shouted Matt. "I want to stay here with Jessie. Can't you understand?"

"The contract on the house runs out in January, so we have to go then whatever happens. Be reasonable, Matt."

His mother looked tired; she always looked tired

now. Caught between Matt and his father, she seemed unable to do anything right any more, and because of this she was beginning to hate the black puppy which followed Matt as though he were some sort of god. We were happy before, she thought.

Three

IT was a cloudy day at the end of August when Joe Clay heard the yard bell ring. His wife was working in the back while he was checking show entries. He went to the gates and found a tall slim woman waiting with a young Labrador standing beside her. It was Matt's mother and Jessie.

"I wondered whether you would like her," she said, pointing at Jessie and taking off dark glasses to look at Joe. "We don't want any money, just a good home. We are going away in the New Year and I think she should have a new home before she's too old to settle down, don't you?"

"Wouldn't be a bad thing," said Joe Clay, kneeling to look at Jessie, then seeing the white patch under her chin.

Jessie backed away from him, for in the dim recesses of her brain she was remembering something unpleasant about this man, something which spelled danger. She pulled at her lead and whined, her tail between her legs, her eyes pleading to be taken home.

"We don't want any money," Matt's mother repeated. "My son found her nearly drowned in a sack. I wish we could keep her, but we are going away," she said again. "I think she must be pedigree, don't you? She looks pure bred."

"Yes, she's a good bitch: there's no doubt about that," agreed Joe Clay.

"My son calls her Jessie. You will find her a good home, won't you?"

"The very best, madam," said Joe Clay. "Do you want the lead back?"

"Yes please, because we may get another dog one day," she said.

Joe Clay had to drag Jessie through the gate before he turned to lock it, while Matt's mother hurried home across the water meadows. The sun was setting. Matt had gone to London with his father. They would be back soon. The last thing he had said to his mother was: "Look after Jessie."

But his father had told her, "I want Jessie gone when I return. All right?" Now as she hurried home she was telling herself that she had done the right thing. She had taken Jessie to the best kennels for miles, where she would be well looked after until Mr. Clay made a profit by selling her to a good home. But what else could she do? It was better than having the dog put down. And now they could settle down to being the happy family they had been before, with no more chewed shoes or chair legs. And when Matt was older and they were settled for good, they would buy him any dog he wanted and he could keep it for ever.

"Eileen, come here a minute. Look who's here," called Joe Clay. His wife came grumbling from the back. "What do you want another Labrador for? Haven't we got enough?" she asked.

Joe Clay lifted Jessie's nose. "Look at that," he said. "She's come home again."

"What are you going to do with her? We can't keep her."

"Find her a home. We won't say she came from here," he said. "We'll ask a hundred for her and if we can find someone who doesn't know the rules," said Joe, "we'll make a little money that way, Eileen— enough for a day at the seaside."

"More than enough," said Eileen.

They had to drag Jessie to a pen which had a concrete run and a wooden bench covered with straw under a tin roof. The other dogs were barking now. Joe Clay let Jessie go and she sat with her neat black nose pressed against the bars, waiting for Matt to appear and take her home.

Matt was thinking about Jessie, but he did not tell his father because his father did not like him talking about Jessie. He even hated the photographs Matt had put in an album with *Jessie* written on the outside. It was an album which started with Jessie at a few weeks old. Anne was in some of the photos too; it was to be a record of Jessie's life until Matt went to the USA. But now he talked to his father about the wonderful day they had had together in London, about the trip they had enjoyed on the river from

Charing Cross to Greenwich, about seeing the Prime Minister walking into the House of Commons, and about the crush in the Underground.

"I'm glad I don't live in London, Dad. But I enjoyed going there," he said politely, imagining Jessie waiting at the door, her leaps of welcome and the feel of her tongue on his hand. She was always the same. Even when he was tired and flustered, her welcome never changed.

"It's been a lovely day, Dad," Matt continued as they stepped out of the train. "Thank you for taking me; it will be something to talk about when I get back to school. The pigeons were fantastic in Trafalgar Square and I'm glad I don't have to be a sentry standing so still all day: it must be terrible. Supposing you wanted to scratch your nose?" He was talking faster and faster because suddenly his father seemed so silent, as though something was wrong . . . as though Matt had done something wrong; that's how it felt anyway . . .

"I'm glad you enjoyed it, Matt."

The car was in the station car park. The sun was setting over the small town, burnishing the slated roofs with gold. The leaves on the trees were turning yellow; soon they would be falling on the dull grey pavements . . .

In ten minutes they would be home. Mum would have a meal waiting; it would be like every other evening in the old, enchanted house they had rented, where the garden smelt of roses and the apples were ripening on the apple trees, and the lawn stretched emerald green to where it met the paving stones of the patio which led to the French windows of the sitting room. Whatever happened in the future, it would be the house which would always make Matt remember Jessie . . .

Harassed businessmen were hurrying to their cars or to the nearby hotel for a quick drink before returning home.

"What will school be like in America?" Matt asked. "I mean, will it be like an English one?"

"You'll learn American history instead of English history, and I believe you have to salute the American flag every morning and swear allegiance, but I may be wrong," his father said, starting the engine.

Matt's mother had made his favorite dish. She had put a bag of crisps ready for him on the table in the hall and the biggest bar of chocolate she could find. But she knew it was not enough: nothing would be enough to replace Jessie. She was missing Jessie herself and, although she had removed the dog basket from the kitchen, it still seemed to be there waiting for her. For the first time in her life she was dreading Matt's arrival and, though she had rehearsed her explanation, she knew that it still wasn't good enough.

The car stopped. Matt leapt out. "What's the hurry?" asked his father.

"Nothing. No hurry. I'm not hurrying," shouted Matt, already running towards the house.

His mother was standing in the doorway with red-rimmed eyes, looking miserable and guilty at the same time. Matt stopped in his tracks. There was no Jessie rushing forward to meet him, her eyes alight with love, her tail wagging, strange whines coming from deep in her throat. It was as though there had been a death in the house—just a silence and his mother's face.

"Where's Jessie? She's dead, isn't she?" shouted Matt. "You let her out and she got run over."

Afterwards his mother was to wonder why she had not said, "Yes, that's right. She's dead." It would have saved so many problems. But she had been taught to tell the truth. "Beauty is truth, truth beauty," her mother had told her over and over again, and it was something she had never forgotten.

So she said, "I've found her a home, Matt, or rather she's gone to somewhere where they will find her a really good home, Matt darling. I didn't *want* to do it. It was being cruel to be kind. After ten months or a year, dogs don't settle so well and she would never have forgotten you, Matt. You wouldn't have wanted her pining for you, would you, darling?"

She could not bear to look at his face.

"So that's why Dad took me to London. It was all a plot. Thank you very much—very clever," Matt said, and hardly knew his own voice for the bitterness of it.

"She's only a dog, Matt. As your mother said, it's no kindness keeping her month after month, because the moment had to come in the end," his father told him.

And his mother held out a bar of chocolate as though that could heal his anguish—a bar of chocolate in exchange for Jessie!

"I don't want any supper. I don't want *anything*," he said in a voice trembling on the verge of tears. "I don't want to sit with you, or eat with you, or to watch television with you. I don't want to speak to you," and now he could feel tears cascading down his face. "We are not going till January. You could have *waited*. Something would have turned up. Someone we knew would have taken Jessie. Now I shall never see her again." He pushed his fists into his eyes to stop the tears.

His mother was crying too now, while his father shouted, "I never thought I would see such a fuss over a dog. Grow up. Be your age, Matt."

"I've never had an animal until now," cried Matt. "She was my first and you had to give her away. You didn't even have to pay for her."

"It was for her own good."

"I would have found her a home . . ."

"You kept saying that."

He ran upstairs, slammed his bedroom door after him and locked it. The room had belonged to Jessie too. Her photo was by his bed in a frame he had bought from Woolworths. Her brush and comb were on a table; only her lead was missing, and of course Jessie herself.

The room felt dead without her. Matt could hear his parents talking downstairs; his father saying, "Come and have a glass of sherry. He will get over it. You did the right thing. Let's have a little sanity. In a month he will have forgotten all about her, you'll see."

But Matt knew it was not true, for he would never forgive his parents for what they had done. Nor forget

Jessie. And whatever they said, he would find her, or she would find him, because they could not manage without each other . . . As Matt lay on his bed he was already making plans, plans to find her, to hide her, to keep her somehow till January, or even beyond.

Four

MATT could not sleep, and when he did his dreams were of Jessie. His parents had vainly tried to persuade him to eat. But the day he had spent in London with his father had become one of treachery, and now he felt he would never forgive them for what they had done. They seemed to have plotted against him, so that, while he was enjoying himself, Jessie was being dragged away to a new life, without a chance for him to say goodbye. The thought made him cry harder than ever so that soon his pillow was wet with tears. It brought dreams so terrible that he was awake before dawn, pacing his small bedroom, his mind crying, "What can I do? I must do *something*. I can't let her go without even a goodbye." And then at last he had an answer—he must find Jessie and run away with her. He could pretend he was sixteen and find a job. He could stand on his own feet and support Jessie and himself.

Then, like a gift, he knew where his mother must have gone with Jessie. She had gone to the nearest place, to the kennels on the hill. Her car had been in for service yesterday, so she would have had to have gone somewhere near, and there was nowhere else. And if he was quick he would find Jessie before she was sold. So he emptied the money out of his money box. It came to three pounds and fifty pence, which was not much but enough, he thought. He pulled on jeans, a T shirt and a sweater before finding a jacket, because it would be a cold night. Then, putting a flashlight and the money in his pocket, he looked round his room and said goodbye. It was only a rented room, but because of Jessie the best he had ever lived in—the only one he would remember when he was old and grey, if he lived that long. He found Jessie's lead outside on the banisters where his mother had left it.

Dawn had broken as he slipped silently downstairs and unlocked the back door. Birds were singing in the trees; rabbits ran from the lawn; cobwebs thin as gossamer joined the flowers together. The milkman was walking up the road outside, whistling. Otherwise there was no one to be seen, though from the fields came the sound of rough bovine tongues on lush grass. And from somewhere, far away, came the whinnying of a horse. Like his mother the day before, Matt walked across the water meadows, where a mist hovered still above the stream and the willow branches hung low above the water. His feet grew wet in his shoes and, because he had eaten nothing the night before, sharp pangs of hunger attacked his stomach.

The kennels were on the side of a trunk road which the oldest locals still called "the turnpike." There was a notice outside which read PUPPIES FOR SALE, another which read BOARDING KENNELS AND CATTERY, and a small one which told you to ring the bell for attention.

It was very quiet inside and the iron gates outside were locked. Matt looked at the locked gates, while cars and trucks thundered by in an unceasing stream and nearby a cock started to crow fit to burst his lungs.

The gate wasn't hard to climb to a keen tree-climber and Matt moved swiftly, his heart pounding like a sledgehammer against his ribs. Seconds later he landed silently on the paved ground yard and ran forward, doubled up like a soldier fearing gunfire. Then he could see Jessie alone in a pen, pressed hard against the bars, waiting with doleful eyes. She gave a cry of welcome, which was neither a bark nor a whine but something between, and her tail started to wag while her eyes said, "I knew you would come, Matt. I've been waiting." Then he was kneeling against the bars while she licked his hands; and he was holding back the tears which wanted to pour down his face while he told himself that there was no time for sentiment, that like a soldier he had a job to do, and that was to save Jessie.

He shot back the bolt on her pen, then slipped on her lead while she squirmed at his feet, professing her joy at seeing him again. He found another way out, a gate into fields which led to the road. As he ran with Jessie he was still doubled up. She thought it was a game and frolicked as she ran, snapping at her lead.

They stood on the road, the boy and the dog, and

Matt imagined his parents waking up and going to his room, his mother shouting, "Maurice! Matt's gone. His room's empty."

He did not feel guilty, because they had betrayed Jessie. He thought, let them suffer. Then he thought of Anne waking up in the next modern house at the end of "The Close" where she lived. He had thought of inviting her to join him, but she would have been another liability and her father might have involved the army, because a girl missing sounded far worse than a boy. Matt thought his parents would guess he had Jessie with him, and know that with her he would be safe.

It was morning now and his stomach was shouting for food while his legs felt weak. Then a truck stopped and a beefy man leaned down to ask, "Do you want a lift, son?" He nodded and climbed up with Jessie following . . .

"Where are you going then?" asked the driver.

Matt answered without thinking, "Oxford."

"I'll drop you on the City Centre road then," said the driver. "Seeing someone, are you?"

Matt nodded and was glad he had not said London, which might have raised the man's suspicions. Oxford was the nearest large town. "An aunt, actually," Matt added, surprised how easily he could lie.

"Nice dog you've got there. Looks pedigree," said the driver next.

"She is, except for the white under her chin," Matt answered.

The driver passed him a bag of sweets. "Help yourself," he said, and Matt took an orange one. He remembered how often his parents had said, "Never accept lifts from strange men. Never take sweets from strangers." But he knew he ought to be all right with Jessie, who was now sitting beside him, looking out of the window as though travelling high up in a truck was something she did every day! No one will abduct me with Jessie; they wouldn't dare, Matt thought.

"How old are you then?"

"Nearly sixteen."

"You don't look it," the driver said. "You look more like eleven to me. I shouldn't thumb lifts if I were you. It could be dangerous."

"I'm small for my age," replied Matt, looking ahead along the straight road. Now he could see spires in the distance, and a whole city.

"How will you get back?" the driver asked.

"My mum will pick me up," Matt said.

Soon they had reached a roundabout and the driver leaned forward to open the cab door. "You'll have a mile's walk, but it's the best I can do, son," he said. "Go carefully now."

Matt refused all further lifts and walked along the rubbish-strewn verge. For a time the spires grew no nearer, while the sky cleared and was suddenly a cloudless blue without a quiver of wind. The grass was tired and contaminated with fumes from the huge trucks which roared past in an endless convoy, while on the faster lanes the cars zigzagged, passing and repassing, most of the drivers grim-faced. Jessie walked bravely, though in her heart she only wanted to return home, to lie in her own bed and recover from the fear she had felt in Joe Clay's kennels. She could not understand why they were walking along the dirty grass in the heat, farther and farther away from home, but if Matt had wished she would have followed him to the ends of the earth. So she walked on, with her tail down and her ears back, not arguing, just longing to turn back.

At last they reached the town. Matt bought chocolate and crisps and they sat on a seat in St. Giles. Matt shared the food equally and the sun lit the spires with gold and all the traffic in the world seemed to be passing by . . .

"At least you are not in kennels any more," Matt told Jessie. "But I wish we could go home. I don't know where to go or what to do. I only know I *had* to find you."

Jessie stared at the traffic and her paws were dusty and her eyes were sad. "You want to go home too. Home? Go home?" Matt asked. Jessie wagged her tail and, jumping up, licked his face, not once, but over and over again. "Sit. Sit down," cried Matt, pushing her down. "We *can't* go home. It isn't safe. Try to understand."

"Matt's gone. Maurice, are you listening? Matt's *gone*," cried Matt's mother. "His room is empty!"

"Don't be silly. He's gone for a walk, and why not? It's a lovely morning." Matt's father was shaving. It was seven-thirty A.M. "You mustn't panic so," he said. "He *is* nearly eleven now."

She went outside and, looking down the road, called, "Matt, are you there? *Matt* . . . ?"

41

"He *never* gets up before nine in the holidays," she called up the stairs. "He's run away because of Jessie." Her face was haggard with worry. "I have to be at work at nine. What are we going to do?"

"He'll turn up. He's probably gone to see Anne," said Matt's father, pulling on his trousers.

"At seven-thirty in the morning?"

"Yes, why not? I can't stay home waiting for him. I've got an important meeting at eleven this morning." Matt's father always had important meetings. He put his work first and his family second, because, as he was always saying, without his earnings they would not survive. "Go on to work as usual. He'll be back by lunchtime," he said next, tipping breakfast cereal into a bowl. "He's not a kid any more. He's old enough for some sense. When *I* was eleven . . ."

Oh, no, not that again, thought Matt's mother, rushing into the kitchen. When he was eleven *he* had had his own business, was selling anything he could get hold of, was making money hand over fist . . . She had heard it all time and time again.

Matt had found a meadow now. Bright with ragwort, it stretched for miles right down to the river. There were cows and horses grazing there, hearty people walking dogs, and boats on the river. Matt sat with Jessie looking at the river, which was wide and hardly moving. Swans swam majestically on the water while ducks quacked merrily to one another like people at a party. Some horses stood head to tail swishing at the flies with long tails, and some of the cows were standing in a shallow stretch of river, while from the town there came the chiming of bells. Matt dozed by the river and Jessie lay panting at his feet. He had made no plans beyond running away with her.

He had no idea how they would live. And now Jessie was restless and kept standing up and saying plainly with her eyes, "It's time to go home." Then the sky started to cloud over. There were ominous rolls of thunder, the cows left the river and the horses moved away seeking shelter.

The people who had been walking or running in the meadow turned for home, and men in a rowing boat turned it round to head for the town. Jessie started to bark, running away from Matt and then returning, licking his hands, wagging her tail desperately, pleading with her eyes.

"All right, we'll go back to the town," Matt said, leaping to his feet. Then the thunder rolled nearer and the sky grew dark as night before lightning flashed like sudden sunlight in his eyes. Jessie ran ahead, waited for him, then ran on. Rain fell in fat angry drops, isolated like drips from a leaking tap. The thunder grew nearer. The horses had reached the shelter of a hedge. The cows stood clustered together. Matt remembered his father saying, "Never shelter under a tree in a storm; that's the way to get struck by lightning."

Rain was falling faster now. The thunder, when it came, seemed to rock the earth, and the lightning lit up the dark sky with quick darting flashes as bright as a flash of gunfire. I'm *not* frightened, Matt told himself, and could feel his heart pounding against his ribs. The ragwort bent before the storm; rain fell faster and faster in a deafening rush. It soaked Matt's clothes in seconds and flattened Jessie's coat. It was as though the heavens were emptying their lakes on the meadow. Then at last Matt and Jessie reached a street running with water. The rolls of thunder grew fainter, until they sounded no more than distant gunfire . . .

Matt put Jessie's lead on. Rain ran through his clothes onto the pavement; his hair dripped onto his face. If only the sun would return and dry us, he thought, but the sky was still dark and the thunder continued to rumble like an angry beast growling in his den . . .

Matt stood in a shop doorway with Jessie, and a man said, "You look wet. Why don't you go home? You'll get your death of cold standing there in those wet clothes."

"I have to wait for a bus," Matt lied.

"No buses come this way son," replied the man looking at him curiously. "The thunder will come back. It always does; it runs backwards and forwards along the river. The storm isn't over yet." He was a tall thin man with an old-fashioned mackintosh turned up round his ears, his hair short like a soldier's or a policeman's.

"You can come home with me if you like," he said next. "I'll fix you something to eat. I've got some nice meat, and ice cream in the fridge. You look famished. Your dog can have a bone too. I've got one for making soup, but I don't mind—she can have it . . . I don't need soup. And you both look famished," he repeated, touching Matt's arm. "Come along, don't argue." Matt felt danger, while a snarl lay low in Jessie's throat . . .

"It's all right, thank you. We're going to get our bus now," Matt said.

"I will take you home. Where do you live? Come and have something to eat. You look starved. We can have it in a restaurant if you like." He took Matt by the arm. "We'll make a run for it." His fingers were long and they bit into Matt's arm.

"No thank you," Matt shouted. "No thank you . . ." and he could hear the panic in his voice echoing in his ears. Then Jessie raised her voice and the snarl in her throat turned into a growl so vicious that the man released Matt's arm and Matt started to run down a long street. But he knew the man was following, walking fast, his feet steady and even on the wet pavement. Matt hauled Jessie after him into a telephone booth and the door slammed shut . . . He looked at the list of codes framed on the wall and dialled home, but all he could hear was the engaged tone repeating itself over and over again. His heart was thumping and he thought, Mum's ringing the police, but she's going to be too late because I'm going to be kidnapped. Jessie looked through the glass at the man outside, her lips drawn back in an angry snarl. Matt put down the receiver and then tried again. And as the traffic roared by he thought, I could scream but no one would hear me . . .

Matt's mother had returned from work. She had

been ringing the house on and off for two hours and had left work early. She had rung Anne's and James' mothers, and she had tried to ring Matt's father, but his secretary had said he was out and could not be reached before two o'clock. So now she was ringing her brother, her only relative still alive, who lived in London and loved birds as some people love children.

Anne was searching the fields for Matt and James had set out on his bike to scour the town. They had both assured her that Matt would never do anything silly, that he was old for his age and sensible, but she was in such a panic she felt it was not true.

Her brother Eric was at home bathing the leg of a pigeon rescued from Trafalgar Square. "Hullo, Sis, what a surprise," he cried, still clutching the pigeon, and for once she did not say, "Don't call me Sis: you know I hate it." Instead she told him about Matt and Jessie and finished, "If he turns up at your place, ring me for God's sake, Eric. I'm at my wit's end." And Eric said, "Not to worry, he's a great kid: he'll return all right. But listen, Sis: I'll have Jessie while you are away. Tell him that . . . I know how he feels. I always wanted a pet when I was a kid."

"But we are away for a whole year," cried Matt's mother.

"That's all right, no problem. I'll walk her on the common every morning. Not to worry . . . But ring the police if he's not home by nightfall; don't forget," said Eric . . . "Good luck . . . And remember, I'll have Jessie."

The man was still there when Matt opened the door. He looked at Matt and smiled. "No luck? No bus? No transport? I'll run you home. No problem. Or are you a runaway?" he asked, putting his head on one side and looking at Matt. "Here, give me your hand," he said.

Matt put his hands in his pockets.

"Come on. Do as you're told, my lad," said the man. "Don't disobey your father."

"You're not my father. And if you touch me my dog will tear your heart out," said Matt, returning to the booth with Jessie, wedging his foot against the door, dialing home again . . . praying that his mother would be there.

This time she answered and Matt shouted, "It's me. I've got Jessie. I'm in a telephone booth in Oxford and there's a man outside trying to kidnap me . . . What shall I do?"

"Stay where you are. Where are you exactly?" she cried, her voice shrill with anxiety.

Matt looked round. "There's a notice outside which says *St. Aldate's*," he answered, "and the Post Office is quite near."

"Scream if he touches you. I'll be with you in twenty minutes. Be careful now. Don't go away . . ." she said and Matt knew that she was crying. "Don't drive too fast, Mum," he said, imagining a pile-up with his mother in the middle of it . . . "Don't rush. I will be all right. Jessie is with me. Don't worry, Mum. Drive carefully . . ."

"Stay where you are whatever happens. Don't let him touch you . . ." cried his mother, putting down the receiver.

She could not find the car keys, could not find her bag. The rain was falling in torrents, but she had heard from Matt, and Jessie's future was settled, so in spite of the rain she felt as though she had emerged from a dark wood into sunlight.

A woman knocked on the booth door and said, "Are you going to be there much longer? I've been waiting ten minutes."

The tall man had drifted away, but it could be just a ploy to get Matt out into the open again, and because of that Matt was not moving from the booth until he saw his mother in her bright red car.

"I can't move," he said.

"You can't shelter from the rain in a telephone booth. I've been waiting ten minutes to phone," the woman repeated. "I'll fetch a policeman if you don't come out."

"I'm not coming out: you'll have to go somewhere else," Matt said. "This isn't the only telephone, I bet there's some in the Post Office."

"Dogs aren't allowed in the booths either," she told him before turning away, plump pink legs wobbling above high heels.

The cars outside were hardly moving. The rain had stopped. Matt pretended to be telephoning. A young man tapped on the window. "How much longer are you going to be?"

"I don't know."

"I've got an important call to make."

"So have I," Matt said.

He dialled Anne's number and pushed in some money. "It's me, Matt," he said.

"Where *are* you?" she shrieked. "Your mother's mad with anxiety. How could you *do* it?"

"She's on her way to fetch me."

"Have you got Jessie?"

"Yes, she's here with me."

"James is looking for you too. Another hour and your Mum would have rung the police. Is Jessie all right?"

"I hope so." He looked at Jessie: she was bedraggled and looked downhearted, but he only had to say her name and her eyes brightened. "She's all right," he said.

Then he could see his mother stuck in a traffic jam, her hair damp against her head, her hands clenched to the steering wheel as though it were a life raft in a stormy sea. "Mum's here, bye." Jessie ran with him. He shrieked "Mum!" Another minute and he was pushing Jessie into the back of the car and leaping in after her.

"You're wet," his mother said. "Where's the man?"

"Gone . . ."

"You gave me such a fright . . . Don't ever do it again, Matt, do you hear? Don't ever do it again . . ."

"I'm sorry. Have we got to take Jessie back?" Matt's hand was through Jessie's collar and it was trembling.

"No, she's going to Eric while we're away; it's all fixed up."

"To Eric?"

"Yes."

"But he's weird!" Matt said.

"He loves animals and that's what counts," his mother answered.

"I only wanted to save Jessie," Matt said. "I didn't want to run away."

"I know."

Five

"SO you're keeping Jessie until January?" Anne asked.

They were sitting by the stream where they had found Jessie. "Is your Uncle Eric all right—suitable? You know what I mean," she said, her bare feet dabbling in the water.

"I expect so, but I've only seen him a couple of times. Dad doesn't like him. They're opposites in everything, but he does love animals."

"It *must* be better than kennels anyway," said Anne cheerfully.

"Except that he lives in London and one year is like seven to a dog. Seven long years of pavements! And he hasn't a whole house, just a flat," Matt said, seeing in his mind a grey pavement, endless traffic, a few small rooms. And Jessie . . .

"You can't expect everything," Anne said.

"He never writes letters; he's too busy rescuing sick pigeons, so I won't get any letters," Matt grumbled.

He had discussed the arrangement with his mother. His father would not talk about Jessie any more. He was still furious at Matt running away. He had wanted to spank Matt, only his mother had prevented it, standing between them, her fists clenched, her eyes bright with tears. But Matt had no intention of telling Anne this, because to be spanked at his age was too humiliating to mention.

"My parents go to Belize at the end of November. Then I start at my new school and spend the holidays with Granny," Anne said. Matt was hardly listening. He was remembering Jessie returning home. She had rolled over and over on the lawn and rushed up and down stairs and through the hall, scattering mats in a wild ecstasy of joy. She had leapt on Matt's bed, and wrinkling back her lips had laughed at him. She had lain upside down asking for her tummy to be stroked.

Since that day she had done everything asked of her with a new alacrity, as though being sent away was some kind of punishment for some sin she had committed; almost as though she was trying to say, "I'm sorry. I won't ever do it again." The thought of leaving her with Uncle Eric was hardly bearable, but he had promised his mother that he would hand Jessie over without a fuss and not discuss the parting any more, and because of this he had been forgiven for running away to Oxford. His mother had talked to Joe Clay on the telephone. Clay had been mystified by Jessie's sudden disappearance. He had searched the fields and nearby woods and accused his wife of not locking the yard gates properly. Matt's mother had ended by sending him ten pounds compensation for the worry Matt had caused. Now as far as she was concerned, the episode was closed, or that is what she said. "Just never run away again, Matt," she said . . .

"Have you heard a word of what I've been saying?" inquired Anne now, laughing.

"Yes, your parents are going to Belize in November," answered Matt, returning to the present.

"Will you write to me at boarding school? I shall want to know about Jessie," said Anne, wiping her wet feet on the long grass.

"Yes, of course, if I remember," answered Matt, only half-listening because he was watching Jessie chasing a rabbit, giving little yaps as she ran.

"You can write to my Granny's address if you like. She lives in London and I shall be going there at half term," Anne said.

Matt returned to school. The autumn was warm and mellow. Soon the leaves lay brown and golden on the grass around the house. Matt's father was busier than ever. His mother was buying clothes for Florida, and Anne was preparing to leave. Matt felt as windswept as the fallen leaves for soon he too would be gone. Often he imagined Jessie in London, threading her way through crowds with a bewildered look in her eyes. He remembered how she had hated walking along the verge near Oxford. However would she stand London? But he had given his word, and there was no going back on it.

Jessie, now almost full grown, seemed to understand every word Matt said to her and her vocabulary grew larger every day. "Bath," "bed," "din dins" and "walkies," she had known for some time, but now she seemed to be listening in on conversations and reacting to them. For instance if Matt said, "Shall we go out after lunch?" she would fetch her lead and put it on his knee, or if a bath was mentioned in any context she would disappear.

At school everyone was talking about exams Matt would never take. Because he would soon be gone the teachers had lost interest in him, so his interest dwindled too.

Anne kissed him quickly on the cheek when she came to say goodbye. "I'll write to you, and make sure you answer," she said.

School was lonelier without her. Matt clung to James now, who was growing so fast that now his trousers barely reached his ankles and the cuffs of his blazer were inches above his bony wrists.

Snow fell in December and Matt's mother started to pack for Florida. Matt sat watching her and she said, "We're going to have our very own swimming pool. Isn't that something, Matt?"

But Matt did not want a swimming pool. He only wanted to keep Jessie. There was nothing in the whole world he wanted as much as that.

A few weeks later his mother told him to start packing. "You can't put it off, Matt. I've washed everything for you," she said, glancing at him with brown eyes which dared him to refuse.

School had ended. Matt had said goodbye to his teachers without regret, for he had never fitted in. Now he said, "But there's still two weeks left, Mum."

"Oh, Matt, two weeks is no time at all. Just do as you are told, okay?" she answered.

The house was half empty because so much had been sent ahead by sea. Jessie could not understand it: things being taken away made her restless, as though she sensed a change for the worse. Because of this she stayed close to Matt, following him from room to room, sitting beside him at meal times, her nose on his knee. Matt still hoped for a sudden change of plans. He even prayed that his father would fall ill, not dangerously, but badly enough to keep him in England. When Christmas came he filled a stocking for Jessie with doggie chocolate drops, a squeaky toy, a ball, a bar of her favorite doggie chocolate and a new brush and comb.

"I want her to have something to take with her when she goes," he told his mother.

"Oh, darling, you make her sound just like a baby; she'll be all right, I promise," she told him, rumpling his hair.

He bought James a digital watch, his mother a book about the United States called *The Greatest Country on Earth*, and his father a pocket calculator. He sent Anne a photograph of Jessie sitting on the garden seat, the white just visible under her chin, her eyes tentative as though asking, "Am I doing the right thing?" He had the same photo by his bed in a leather frame.

Christmas cards arrived in the mail; his mother put up decorations; his father bought a tree. But Matt could not look forward to Christmas as he had in the past, because of leaving Jessie.

"Christmases are wonderful in the States. Much better than here," his mother told him.

"You can't go on mourning the temporary loss of a dog, Matt," his father said. "You'll have her back next year."

"I don't believe it. I don't believe I'll ever have her back. You'll be sent to South America or somewhere. I know you will," Matt answered.

"The days will fly. You'll be so busy at your new school that you'll forget all about Jessie. And think of the sunshine," his mother said, just as though he had never spoken.

His father promised, "We'll go to Disneyland, to San Francisco and Los Angeles. It's going to be the greatest year you've ever had, Matt, believe me." His father was on holiday now and had become more cheerful and relaxed.

Anne sent Matt a Christmas card and Jessie a toy bone. On the card she wrote, *"I hate it here and can't wait to start school. Lucky you—going to America. Give Jessie three big kisses from me. Love, Anne,"* and she added three crosses to signify kisses.

Christmas passed quickly. If it had not been for Jessie, Matt would have felt as lonely as he did most Christmases, without brothers, sisters or grand-parents. Afterwards the weather cleared. The sun shone. Jessie followed Matt like a shadow now, watching him pack, taking the clothes out of his case and putting them on the bed, as softly and proudly as if she were carrying game. The sight made Matt curl up inside and brought tears to his eyes. "It's no use, Jessie," he said. "I've *got* to pack."

She ate her dinner now without enthusiasm. She knew that Matt was leaving for good. So she pleaded with her eyes to be told, "You are coming too." But Matt could not say it. Nor could he bring himself to say, "No, Jessie, you are staying behind," for every time he tried the words seemed to die in his throat.

Soon there was little left in the kitchen besides the fitted units and Jessie's basket. Then the fateful morning arrived when Matt's mother announced, "Eric's arriving tomorrow to collect Jessie."

Jessie seemed to understand and looked at them with such a look of sorrow that Matt fell on his knees before her crying, "It's not for ever, Jessie. I promise you I'll be back next year and then I'll be here for-ever. And a year will soon pass, Jessie." It was almost the same as his parents had said to him and he knew it was not true, because a year of a dog's life is like seven of ours, and seven years is a long time.

"Now, no crying tomorrow, Matt," his father told him sternly. "Because it won't help anyone, least of all Jessie. Besides you are too old to cry. Just think of people going to wars and never coming back, like my father dying in Kenya and my mother dying of grief. Think of that, Matt. Have a sense of proportion, Matt. Get your priorities right and everything else will fall into place."

But Matt had only one priority—Jessie.

The cases they were taking with them were stacked in the hall now. Jessie sniffed at them forlornly. Then Matt brushed her, saying, "You are going to be all right, I promise," and his mother said, "I wish Eric was here now. I wish we could get it over with. But don't worry, Matt, because, though my brother is eccentric, he loves animals, and I know he'll make her happy."

Jessie lay on Matt's bed all that long winter night and no one had the heart to order her off, least of all

Matt. When morning came it was freezing cold, the trees iced with frost, the sky a cold relentless grey. The central heating had been switched off, the boiler let out, because by afternoon the house would be empty. Jessie would be with Eric, Matt and his parents would be winging their way to America.

Still in his pajamas, stroking Jessie, Matt knew there was nothing more he could do and no way out. Only Jessie's toys had to be put ready in her basket along with her brush and comb, and her vaccination certificates in an envelope.

Eric arrived at eleven o'clock in a battered Ford car. He had wild red hair which stood up around his head, while his eyes moved constantly behind gold-rimmed glasses. When he saw Jessie he fell on his knees in front of her and stayed there while she gravely presented him with a paw.

"She's lovely, a real winner. I shall be proud to take her with me," he cried, shaking her neat black paw, the one with two pink claws, and smiling at Matt. Then he stood up and started to tell them about the scarecrow he had invented. Matt saw his father lift his eyes to heaven and sigh and a look of wry amusement come over his mother's face and he knew they were laughing at Uncle Eric inside themselves.

"It's fantastic. It runs on a battery and at regular intervals it rings an alarm bell and swings its arms. You can set it to switch off at a certain time, and with luck a battery lasts a week at least. I'm going to make a fortune; I know I am," explained Eric.

"Oh, Eric, we've heard it all before," said Matt's mother.

"Maybe, but this time it's going to be different. I've sold ten already. They're dirt cheap. I go round the farms selling them. Jessie can come with me; she'll love it."

Uncle Eric would not stay long. "You want to be off, and I've got some farms to visit on the way back," he told them, thinking he had better take Jessie quickly for Matt's sake, like a clean cut with a knife: no sense in prolonging the agony.

He drank a large mug of coffee with three big gulps; then wiped his mouth with the back of his hand. "Mustn't waste time. I'll leave a leaflet with you. Maybe you can sell 'Eric's Scarecrow' in the United States," he suggested laughing, his eyes darting behind his glasses.

"Is that what it's called?" asked Matt.

"That's right. Nice and simple. Anyone can say it. And it's only sixteen pounds a go. Anything comparable costs twenty-eight pounds upwards. I put them together myself, three or four a day sometimes," continued Eric as he clipped Jessie's lead to her collar. "Come on, old girl, time to go," he added, leaning down to pat her sleek black sides. "You're going to live with Uncle Eric." He tried to drag her out of the house. She turned to look at Matt, her eyes imploring and unbelieving at the same time. Then with a quick twist she wriggled out of her collar and, dashing past Matt, fled upstairs to his room.

"Go and fetch her, Matt," shouted his father.

Matt took the collar and lead from Uncle Eric without a word; then, reaching his room, knelt near Jessie who had taken refuge under his bed and said,

"I'm sorry, Jessie. You've got to go, but you'll be coming back, I promise," and he could feel the salty taste of tears in his throat. He buckled the collar on her neck and led her downstairs. She followed him with her tail between her legs looking neither right nor left, doing what she was told though it was breaking her heart . . .

"Get in the car with her, Matt . . ." His father was standing outside. Uncle Eric was already in the driver's seat waiting. Jessie's basket was in the trunk; his mother turned away, with her hands over her face, not looking . . .

"I can't," answered Matt.

"You can. All this fuss over a dog. It's pathetic," exclaimed his father.

Jessie followed Matt into the car; then turned to lick his face and he knew she was thanking him because she thought that he was going with her. It touched a raw nerve somewhere inside him and brought a sudden rush of unwanted tears, which he tried desperately to hide from his father.

"Now get out the other side."

Matt kissed Jessie quickly and she started to lick his hands, his face, any part of him she could reach. She licked the tears off his hands and off his cheeks. She thought he was going with her. She thought everything was going to be all right, that he was going to keep her . . . She put her paws on his chest the better to lick his face.

"Get out at once," shouted Matt's father. "Do as I say."

"Best do what you're told, old chap," said Uncle

Eric. "No point in prolonging the agony. She'll be all right when you're gone."

"I can't. I can't do it to her," said Matt.

"You must," replied Uncle Eric quietly.

"Be good. Don't do anything silly. Goodbye, Jessie," whispered Matt hoarsely, struggling free from her, then jumping out into the cold winter air, slamming the car door after him, not looking at his father, nor his mother, not looking back, just shouting over his shoulder, "Don't forget to change her name disc, Uncle Eric." Then he fled to his near empty bedroom and threw himself onto his stripped bed thinking, "I've betrayed Jessie . . ."

Now he could hear his mother calling, "Goodbye, Eric. Thanks a million. Go carefully now. Best of luck." And the cronky old car was leaving with a stuttering from the exhaust and a rattle from underneath and with it Jessie . . . Jessie whom he loved more than anything else in the whole world.

Six

JESSIE sat looking out of the car window, knowing that she was being taken away from Matt and the only home she had ever known. Eric knew how she felt, for he had once loved a woman and been rejected, and the pain was still there so strong that he had never desired another woman. He kept talking to Jessie, saying nothing in particular, just talking. "You will like it with me. I promise you that," he said. "And it won't be forever, Jessie. Matt will come back. He has given his word of honor, Jessie, and won't forget."

And though Jessie knew nothing of honor and could not recognize the words, she sighed and lay down, curling herself into a tight ball. Eric knew then that in her doggy way she had decided that for the moment there was no hope. She had not given up completely, but she was waiting for the situation to change.

They stopped at two farms, but Jessie refused to leave the car and Eric was thankful to leave her there, knowing that she needed time to adjust to her new life.

Eric lived in London in a basement room two minutes' walk from Lasbrook Common. It was the last day of December, and as they reached London people were already celebrating the end of the old year. In Lasbrook Road the street lights were on and there was a roar of traffic as relentless as waves breaking against a sea wall.

Eric took Jessie's basket inside, down the steps and past the garbage cans, putting it down to unlock the solid old-fashioned door which had once led to the kitchen and servants' hall and now led to his home. Chaos reigned inside. There was just a bed-sittingroom which stretched the width of the tall Edwardian house, and at the back a small kitchen and a cramped bathroom. Eric was one of those people who do not care about their surroundings, so he merely stepped over the letters on the doormat and the dirty mugs strewn everywhere, finding a space for Jessie's basket before fetching her from the car. "This is your new home, Jessie," he said. Then, opening a door which led directly to a small dusty garden, he added, "You see, Jessie. Not quite what you're used to, I fear, but the best I can do, old girl."

Jessie was soon in her basket, for now it was the only part of her old home left. She refused to respond to Eric's overtures and turned her nose up at the food he offered. Later, when he took her for a late walk on Lasbrook Common, he kept her on a lead. She followed him tail down, occasionally jumping with fright at the bangs of the distant New Year's Eve fireworks. They looked a strange couple: Eric with his hair on end, in frayed jeans, dark donkey jacket and boots with broken laces knotted together, and the sad black Labrador who followed him so listlessly.

Even though it was so late, there were other dogs being walked on the common—a Pekinese, a spaniel, two mongrels and an enormous Irish wolfhound. None of them interested Jessie, for she was still mourning Matt—and might for weeks yet, thought Eric looking down at her. What we do to animals, he thought. We behave like gods and then desert them. That's humanity for you! For Eric had never got on with his fellow men. A peculiar small boy in glasses, he had been laughed at when at school. His parents had despaired of him. He was one of those people who are never in tune with a conversation, with no natural graces; who trip going upstairs and press the wrong button in lifts; who bang into people in a crowded street, upset coffee on polished tables and sit at reserved tables in restaurants. In other words, a misfit! For a long time Eric had tried to get on with the rest of humanity, but in the end he had turned to animals for company, and in particular to the pigeons in Trafalgar Square. And now to Jessie.

So later when he bent over Jessie to say goodnight and she turned her head away, pressing it more tightly against her haunches and then covering it with her tail, he told her, "Matt's not worth it; no human is. They are not to be trusted. Pass the message round, Jessie: humans are no better than anything else, I would say. They are not worth breaking your heart over, Jessie, not even Matt . . . He's not worth it."

Matt was in a plane now, flying farther and farther from Jessie, desperately trying to put the parting from his mind.

"A year will pass quickly," his mother said. "In no time at all you will be fetching her again. Eric loves animals. He always has. Years ago he set up his own society for the protection of town pigeons. It came to nothing, of course; none of his efforts do. Poor Eric. But animals love him—there's no doubt about that."

"I think he should be sent to a training center, or should attend evening classes on Business Studies. He always looks such a mess. If he dressed better, people would take him more seriously. All his clothes look secondhand," said Matt's father.

"But they are, darling! They come from charity shops," Matt's mother said.

The captain was speaking now, telling them that they would soon be landing in Miami, talking about the temperature, hoping they had had a good journey. Jessie seemed miles away now. As Matt fastened his safety belt, he seemed to belong to another life already, and below lay a whole new world. Matt thought, she'll be all right. I can stop worrying. Eric will look after her . . . He could see light below now, a whole city, and now they were turning, coming in to land. And Jessie seemed no more than a small episode in Matt's life now—just a dog, as his father said, and what's a dog when you are landing in a new world, stepping out onto hot earth in the middle of winter?

What's a dog after all?

A week passed. Jessie started to accept Eric. They travelled to the country together and Jessie sat on the back seat of the battered old Ford while Eric tried to persuade farmers to buy his scarecrows. Many of them admired Jessie, guessing that she was pedigree—"good enough for Cruft's," one said.

They spent so much time in the car that it became like a second home to Jessie, and when they were not in the car or walking on the common they would catch a bus to Trafalgar Square and rescue damaged pigeons. Eric had a special basket to take them home in, and he kept them until they were cured, when he returned them to the Square.

There were other people in the flats above the basement, but they did not speak to Eric, not even to pass the time of day when they went to their cans in the basement area. They told each other that he was mad and that his place smelt of pigeon mess and, worse still, he now had a dog, which spent pennies in the garden. If he had smartened himself up as Matt's father wanted they might have accepted him, but the flats above were expensive, with beautiful bay windows and elegant Edwardian doors. The people who lived there were beautiful too, with wonderful fitted kitchens and rugs from Harrods and clothes from expensive shops, and they considered that Eric lowered the tone of the house.

In the evenings when the other residents were at parties or watching television, Eric put his scarecrows together. Each one was a little different, with a head stuffed with old socks and hair made from cut string, and as he put them together he remembered the sixties, his heyday.

January became February. Jessie followed Eric everywhere with her eyes. She loved him now as she had loved Matt before him. She fell on him in the morning as the alarm clock went off, with licks to any part of him she could reach.

She maddened the other inmates of the house by barking when anyone came to the door. Eric and Jessie travelled miles together through rain and hail and snow, only stopping for Eric to persuade farmers that they would need his scarecrows in the spring. The basement room became full of cold, ancient pigeons. The trees on the common were dripping wet or white with frost. Jessie would run ahead of Eric now to the common, keeping to the pavement, waiting at the crossing. She no longer needed a lead, and the disc which Matt had attached to her collar with her name and telephone number had fallen off, but Eric had not replaced it. Almost every day he thought about it. "Must get you a new disc today, Jessie," he would say. "Don't let me forget. Whine next time we are near a pet shop; don't forget, Jessie," and Jessie would wag her tail, appreciating his words, but not understanding their meaning.

One farmer in Kent even wanted to buy her. "I'll give you fifty, Eric," he said. "A hundred, if you like. My wife's always wanted a Labrador. And you look as though you could do with the money." But Eric shook his head, saying, "No, I don't want to part with her. I appreciate her company too much."

"Your exhaust is hanging off and a new one will cost you a lot," the farmer said, standing squarely in a wet yard, his face glistening red while Eric looked pale and drawn, exhausted by making scarecrows and driving tens of miles to sell each one . . .

"Sorry, she's not for sale," he said.

"It's no life for a dog in London," the farmer called after him.

"She's happy enough. Come on, Jess, we're off," Eric said. "She's not mine anyway. I'm just keeping her for someone else," he called over his shoulder.

He had sold two scarecrows that day, so they stopped at a pub for lunch and made one more call at a farm that afternoon beneath a darkening sky. The farmer, a small man with stained teeth, asked them in, saying, "Sit down and have a bite of something. You look famished and it's bitter cold."

When his wife came down the stairs she made a fuss of Jessie. "I can see you look starved to death. Sit down and I'll get you something hot." The kitchen had clothes steaming on a clothes horse by the Rayburn cooker. A cat sat on a cushion. It was the sort of comfort Eric had not enjoyed in years, and Jessie lay down by the Rayburn, instantly at home.

"I mustn't stay too long. I have to get back to London, and the forecast isn't good," said Eric.

"You need something to set you up," the farmer said. "No good travelling on an empty stomach, and we were just going to eat ourselves, weren't we, Rosie?"

His wife smiled, spreading butter on thick slices of homemade fruit loaf, and Eric felt as though he was a child again. His austere home had not held the same warmth, with the heating switched off all day to save money and the carpets threadbare, but there had been real meals served in a bleak dining room with the table set right and his father correcting his manners as he ate. That was a long time ago and his elderly parents had since died, so that Matt had no grandparents on either side. Yet Eric still missed them, though they had been people who had counted every penny and preached manners and punctuality incessantly.

He lingered on enjoying a mammoth high tea, while all light faded from the sky and an ominous wind rustled the branches of the trees outside. It was half past eight when he and Jessie left the farmhouse, and then the car would not start and had to be pushed out of the farmyard. "Go carefully now," called the farmer, who had bought one of Eric's scarecrows, more from pity than from need. "If ever a man needed looking after, that one does," he muttered, returning indoors.

"Four hours and we will be home," said Eric to Jessie. "It's been a good day, hasn't it? Three scarecrows sold and a good meal into the bargain. We'll go to the supermarket tomorrow and stock up with food. Do you know I've only got one scarecrow left at home? I shall have to make some more."

Jessie wagged her tail and leaned over from the back of the car to lick Eric's face. The farmer's wife had given her a bowl of milk and two cracker biscuits. She had enjoyed sitting in the warm kitchen and would have liked to stay there forever, with Eric of course; but she could not tell him this, so she licked his face to say thank you.

Eric started to sing Beatle songs. He could not sing

in tune, so he never sang unless alone or with Jessie. He had sung less and less lately . . .

They had travelled nearly forty miles when the left headlight failed and the engine started to make a sound like a clucking hen. Eric sang more loudly to blot out his rising fears. "We're not going to break down tonight, definitely not, Jessie," he shouted, though he feared the exact opposite. "The car's going like a bird," he said, though he could feel the engine dying beneath the accelerator, the lights fading and the exhaust spluttering. "Of course we are not going to break down, Jessie, quite impossible," he cried as the engine gave one last splutter and died . . .

Eric managed to steer the car onto the hard shoulder. Luckily they were on a dual highway and the night, though dark, was still dry. "You stay there. I'll get her going again in a jiff, Jessie, not to worry," said Eric, stepping out onto the street.

He threw up the hood, but without a flashlight he could see little: only the odd flash of light from passing cars showed him that the plugs were still in place, the water cap still on, the distributor undisturbed . . . He climbed into the car again.

"We had best wait till morning, Jessie. We'll be all right here, you in your warm black coat and me in my old overcoat which came from Bond Street in the year one. They made things well then, Jessie. It's nearly ten, our bedtime anyway. And in the light of morning I'll mend the old banger or find help. Hey, Jessie, what do you say?"

And Jessie leaned over the seat to lick his hand again; then lay down, her muzzle on one paw, accepting what fate had bestowed on them, content so long as she was with Eric, who had now replaced Matt in her affections to the extent that she would have died for him.

After a time cars stopped passing by and snow fell silently like torn paper from the night sky. Eric shut his eyes and slept, dreaming of scarecrows, each one more beautiful than the last, until one day there was an exhibition of them in a great gallery in London. His friends flocked to see them, the newspapers reported on them, and soon people were stopping Eric in the street to ask, "Are you the man who made all those lovely scarecrows? Congratulations." Old enemies at school wrote to him, and suddenly overnight he was rich and famous.

Jessie was restless. The falling snow worried her, and instinct told her that they should be at home in their lair, not lying exposed at the side of the road. Eric talked in his sleep. So the night passed and the first light of dawn was faint and obscured by falling snow.

Then almost as silent as the falling flakes, a truck-and-trailer travelling swiftly through the dawn skidded on the snow. The trailer swung to the left, hitting Eric's old Ford and crushing the side in before hurling it down the embankment adjoining the hard shoulder and leaving it there, among the dead nettles and grass and the refuse from hundreds of passing cars, crushed beyond recognition.

The truck driver, half-asleep, felt little and saw nothing, and so drove on to his destination untroubled by guilt. Eric knew nothing, saw nothing and did not feel the blood flooding into his ears. Only Jessie lay conscious, imprisoned by the smashed side of the Ford, smelling the blood coming from Eric, dazed, but already overcome by a desire to escape from the wreckage.

Seven

MORNING and daylight came, colder than the night. Jessie whined, and dug into the seat with her paws; then tore at crushed metal with her teeth until her mouth bled. For a time there had been silence; then the sound of a snow plough, of voices calling to one another just above where Eric's car lay crushed. There was no more snow; the sky was almost blue. Help was near, if only Jessie could reach it. She dug on steadily, hearing an involuntary groan from Eric, smelling the blood which had matted his hair and dried around him on the twisted driver's seat. He was alive, but only just.

At last she was free. She went to Eric but it was impossible to do more than lick the almost lifeless hand, still in its glove, which was protruding from the wreckage as if seeking help. Jessie's side and mouth were bleeding as she climbed the bank and reached the hard shoulder again. Cars were passing slowly, travelling in single file along the narrow road made by the snow plough. Jessie stood, her coat dusted with snow from the bank she had climbed, her tail down, her eyes staring towards the oncoming traffic. Instinct had told her she had to find help; instinct now told her to bark. But who would hear a lone Labrador barking against the noise of ever-increasing traffic?

Presently a middle-aged man leaned out of his car window and called, "Good dog. Go home," but he did not dare to stop for fear his car would never start again.

A lady driver made a mental note that she would do something about the black dog when she reached home, but later forgot it . . . Some children shouted, "Look at that dog," to their mother.

"Poor thing, it looks abandoned," their mother answered, driving on.

"Shouldn't we do something about it?" asked the nine-year-old girl.

"Someone will—the police, or some animal society," replied their mother vaguely.

"But what if they don't?"

"Of course they will. We can't stop anyway, darling, because it's so skiddy we'd never get started again, and that would hold up all the traffic."

"I'm sure it's going to die," the girl said.

But Jessie did not die. She went on barking until evening, then returned to the car to sleep as close as she could to Eric, whose face was now the color of putty.

Up on the road, the snow was melting. A warm breeze stirred the night sky, while in distant trees birds thought of spring. The warm night saved Eric: another freezing night would have killed him. Jessie knew that he was still alive and because of that she must go on seeking help when the next day dawned at last. Blood was clotted against her sides and her cut paws had not healed, but she returned to the hard shoulder and started to bark again, her voice hoarse. A drizzle had turned the slush into a river of water. Huge trucks threw up clouds of it as they passed, drenching Jessie. Undaunted, she barked on, until at last a woman in a mini car stopped. "What's the matter, little dog? Come here, you poor wee thing. Are you lost?" she asked, getting out of her car.

Jessie wagged her tail in encouragement, then went a few steps down the bank and returned barking. The woman put on her Wellington boots and followed Jessie. Then looking down the bank she cried, "Oh my God! Oh no, I can't believe it," while Jessie ran on, barking and then looking back, saying plainly, "Follow me."

The woman, Susan Pemberton, looked inside Eric's car, then ran back up the bank. She stood on the roadside waving her arms until another car stopped. "Help! There's a dead man down the embankment. His car is smashed to bits. This must be his dog, poor little thing," she cried. "He must have been there for hours. For God's sake do something!"

"Okay. You stay. I'll go on and phone the police," said the man she had stopped, who wore glasses and a sheepskin coat. "Don't panic. If he's dead we can't do anything anyway . . . Get back in your car and wait," he added before driving off.

Susan Pemberton tried to coax Jessie into her car. But Jessie would not leave Eric, even though Susan caught hold of her collar and pulled until Jessie turned back her lips in a snarl, her eyes suddenly deep pools of anger, a deep growl in her throat.

"All right, stay then," said Susan Pemberton, letting go. "But you will have to leave him in the end, because he's dead." But Jessie, with the instinct of a dog, knew otherwise and sat on the wet grass waiting, her neat ears pricked with expectation. Maybe she imagined them both home again, the warmth from the old-fashioned gas fire drying her coat, Eric in bed wearing his old checked dressing gown. Anyway she waited and, when Susan Pemberton spoke to her again, she looked the other way.

Soon a police car with two policemen in it sped swiftly along the wet road and pulled onto the hard shoulder. "He's down there. You're too late; he's dead," said Susan Pemberton, pointing. "Can I go now? You will look after the dog, won't you? She doesn't want to leave him. She took me to the car, you know. She was barking and barking at the side of the road. You won't just leave her, will you?"

"No way, madam," the younger policeman said.

"I would have her myself if it would help, but I've got three already," explained Susan Pemberton, getting into her car.

"That's all right, Madam. We'll see to the dog, but we would like your name and address, because we may need a statement from you later," the policeman said.

"I don't think the man is quite dead," said the other policeman as he returned up the bank from the crushed car.

Soon there was an ambulance as well as a fire engine, and notices saying SLOW, POLICE, ACCIDENT. The fire engine had to use cutting equipment to free Eric from the wreckage, and all the time Jessie stayed close by waiting to join him when he was free. The policemen tried to make friends with her and called her "Blackie" and "darling", but every time they drew close she moved away.

The ambulance men gave Eric oxygen and, putting him on a stretcher, carried him up the bank to the ambulance. Jessie followed determinedly, her tail down, longing to get near enough to lick the blood off Eric's pale face. It was not until they lifted the stretcher into the ambulance that the younger policeman was able to grab the dog's collar. "You can't go with him. I'm sorry: it's not allowed. Whether you like it or not you've got to come with me," he said.

Jessie struggled and whined as the ambulance drew away, and the policeman had to drag her into the white police car. They left her there while they wrote down the details of the old Ford, noting the state of the tires and the fact that the road tax sign, which was lying on the grass, had run out two months ago. They managed to retrieve Eric's battered briefcase from the wreckage, but all it held was a map, another pair of gold-rimmed spectacles smashed to smithereens, a pen and the addresses of half a dozen farms.

"Not much to go on," they grumbled. "But we will find who he is by the car number, or what remains of it."

They searched in the wet grass for clues to the cause of the accident and noted the skid marks. All the time the radio in their car was giving messages, while Jessie lay curled into a tight ball on the back seat, waiting for Eric to reappear.

"We had better take her to the kennels; it's all we

can do for the time being. They'll look after her until we find his relations," said the elder policeman, who had a beard, three children, and a dog of his own called Rover.

"She saved his life. Do you think he will pull through?" asked the other one, getting into the car.

"He's lucky to be alive. I reckon his skull is cracked and his ribs smashed," replied the older one, starting the engine. "And his breathing sounded very shallow to me."

"I hope he's got some relations for the dog's sake," said the other. "I would hate to think of her being put down after what she's done."

"He must have. We've all got relations somewhere or other. And he's no youngster. He's probably got a missus and half a dozen kids. We'll soon find out anyway," said the bearded policeman, driving swiftly down the dual highway.

Far away in Florida Matt was writing a letter:

'Dear Uncle Eric,' he wrote
'I hope Jessie has settled down now and is happy. I do miss her. I keep seeing dogs like her here, but not as nice. I do hope you are making a million out of your scarecrows. I haven't met any farmers yet, but if I do I will tell them about Eric's Scarecrows. I'm swimming a lot and playing tennis. Please give Jessie the biggest hug in the world from me. Tell her it's not so long now before I'll be back.
Love Matt.'

He folded the letter and put it into an envelope addressed to Uncle Eric in his small neat handwriting.

"I've written to Uncle Eric, so you can't grumble any more, Mum," he called to his mother, sitting beside the swimming pool in a bikini.

"Well done, darling, but don't forget to mail it," she called back.

Matt imagined Eric somewhere in London opening his letter, his strange, excitable, almost haunted face breaking into a smile as he said "Jessie, here's a letter from Matt." I don't suppose he gets many letters, so mine will be a surprise, decided Matt, walking down the hot road looking for a mailbox. Poor old Uncle Eric, he thought: sitting in a cold room in February while we're basking in sunshine.

Suddenly Jessie did not seem quite real, more like something which had happened in a dream or a film. Yet several times Matt had awakened in his spacious American bedroom imagining her tongue on his hand, and then opened his eyes to find she was not there, but thousands of miles away with Uncle Eric. It never failed to upset him; to make him think, if only we were still together. I feel so lost without her, if only, if only. How I hate "if only".

The lady at the kennels, Mrs. Foster, took hold of Jessie.

"Poor little thing, we will look after her," she said.

"We'll let you know the moment we find someone to take her," said the bearded policeman. "There must be a relation somewhere. He wasn't a young chap, forty at least I should say . . ."

"We'll clean her up and keep her for the usual time then," said Mrs. Foster, leading Jessie away to another yard where all around dogs were barking, while other dogs' faces peered through wire mesh, tails wagging, eyes shining with hope; every inmate seeming to be looking for someone.

Jessie's kennel had a concrete floor, a bench with straw on it, and a warm pipe running along the back. It was clean and smelt of disinfectant; there was a bowl of water in one corner and soon a bowl of warm food in another. Later a kennel worker rubbed Jessie with a towel and bathed the cuts on her paws.

"Your master'll be better soon and you'll be all right here, you puir wee thing," she said. "We'll look after you. You have nothing to fear with us, so cheer up. Here, eat your dinner." But Jessie was missing Eric too much to eat anything. In the next kennel a boxer dog sat sad-eyed on his bench, while nearer a small Jack Russell yapped unceasingly.

As soon as the kennel worker had left, Jessie sat against the wire mesh waiting for Eric to rescue her. Her dinner remained uneaten, the water untouched. She was dry and warm now; all she wanted or needed was Eric. She had lost Matt, and recovered. But this time it was different, because Eric had been taken away from her—he had not abandoned her like Matt.

The kennel workers tried to coax her to eat; they called her Gipsy for want of a better name. "Come on, Gip love, eat up, Gip," they said, and every day they walked her round a bare paddock on a lead. They brushed her coat and added vitamins to her food.

They brought her balls and squeaky toys. "If only she would wag her tail," they said.

The boxer was taken away to a new home. The Jack Russell was put to sleep. New inmates arrived while Jessie waited, not knowing her time was limited, that after a month she must be found a new home or die. She waited for Eric, still fighting for his life in a hospital. He had not spoken a word since the accident and might not speak for weeks, if ever again. He was suffering from exposure as well as from a cracked skull, crushed ribs and a broken pelvis, so that it was a miracle that he was still alive. But Jessie did not know this and was waiting for him to turn up calling cheerfully, "Hullo, Jess old girl. We are going home." She dreamed of the apartment in the basement, and sometimes she relived the accident and whined and howled in her sleep. She ate just enough to stay alive and waited, her eyes looking through the mesh with neither hope nor despair in them, just patience.

The police in London had been to Eric's flat. They had interviewed the people above him in the house.

"He had no friends," and "no one ever called to see him. He was a loner, almost a tramp," they said. "No loss to anyone." Yes, they had seen the dog. She barked a lot and woke up the baby in the top flat. They were glad she had gone, and would the flat be able to relet now? "No, he had no steady job," they said. "He was always bringing hurt birds home, and he made some peculiar scarecrows which he tried to sell. His car was a disgrace to the street. It lowered the tone." They were sorry he had had an accident, of course they were, but they didn't want him back; and living in London was no life for a dog, was it?

The police had no time to look further, for what with marches, strikes and pickpockets everywhere they had already spent too long looking for Eric's nearest and dearest. They let themselves into his room and found nothing but bills on the mat and a dying pigeon which they took away with them. Then they moved on to a more important case.

So Jessie waited in the kennels, while in Florida Matt waited for a reply to his letter and February became March, with all the hope March brings in England, with the sap starting to rise in the tired trees and the grass beginning to grow.

"Why hasn't he answered?" complained Matt.

"He's not a letter writer. Some people aren't," his mother said.

"He could have sent a postcard."

"I expect he's busy selling his scarecrows," his mother answered and they laughed, imagining him knocking on farmhouse doors saying, "Do you want a scarecrow, by any chance?"

"Anyway in less than ten months I shall be back in England," Matt said. "And then I shall have Jessie forever and ever . . ."

Eight

"IT'S such a shame," said Jane, the youngest kennel worker. "It would be different if she were old, but she can't be more than a year and that's too young to die . . ."

"And she's so sad for such a young dog," said Sue, who had red hair and striking blue eyes. "But you can't expect the police to pay for her keep for months. Or the taxpayers, come to that."

"I wish I could have her," Jane said. "But we haven't the room, not even a garden. It just wouldn't be fair."

Jessie ignored them, because to be friendly to them was to be unfaithful to Eric, and anyway she saw them as captors rather than friends. Every day she walked listlessly around the exercise field. She ignored the balls they threw, looking in the other direction as though afraid she might be tempted to retrieve them. She picked at her food and lay against the mesh of her run whatever the weather.

"As far as I can see she might just as well be put down," Mrs. Foster said. "Perhaps she got a knock on the head when the car was smashed up. She just doesn't seem normal to me. Pining for a few days is normal, but for a month isn't . . . And she's losing weight too. No one can say we haven't tried, but she just doesn't respond, does she?" She and the kennel workers were drinking coffee in a cluttered kitchen. Dogs were coming in and going out all the time, so what was so special about Gipsy, wondered Jane. Was it that she was so young and so perfect for a Labrador? Or was it her sadness which made you want to cry when you thought that soon she would be put to sleep for ever? And wasn't it true that she was unhappy and would never be happy again without her owner, who the police said might never walk or talk again? And if that was true, surely putting her to sleep was the kindest thing to do?

Tomorrow the vet would be coming in his van to take away the unclaimed and unwanted dogs. Gipsy would go with them unless something happened in the meantime. There were just twenty-four hours left between life and death for Jessie, but she did not know it, was still waiting for Eric, her neat black face pressed against the mesh.

Then, just in time, Mrs. Sanders walked into the yard. She was old and forthright and knew what she wanted. Looking around as though she owned the place, she called out, "Anyone at home? I want a dog, not too big and not too small, a guard dog really."

The two kennel workers took her straight to Jessie. "She's missing her owner, but she's a lovely dog," said Jane, her eyes filling with tears. Other dogs rushed to look out, their eyes lit with hope, looking for owners who had abandoned them, whom they had loved and trusted only to be thrown out when they grew too big to be convenient; dogs whose owners had died, dogs which had bitten the postman thinking that they were protecting their owners' property, dogs which were too boisterous or too nervous, dogs which people had grown tired of looking after. All types: mongrels, cross breds, pure breds; tiny, timid, brave, mousers and ratters, wolfhounds, terriers, spaniels, gun dogs, Alsatians; every breed was there, for the home took in dogs from three counties.

"I want another pedigree dog," said Mrs. Sanders, looking at Jessie. "The last one I had from here—a spaniel—he lived till he was fourteen. But I want something a little bigger now, a sort of guard dog. You see, my husband died last year . . ." She's going to talk forever, thought Jane; we are going to hear her whole life history . . .

"I don't think Gip will be any trouble; she's ever so docile and at your age you don't want a dog which pulls, do you?" she asked.

"I've always wanted a Labrador," Mrs. Sanders repeated. "Yes, I think I will take her. Do you want a contribution? I can't afford a lot, but I expect you'll want something." She went inside to see Mrs. Foster, while the two kennel workers rejoiced.

"I prayed for Gip last night. I can tell you that now," Jane said, leading Jessie out of her run. "So God answered my prayer."

"Or was it a coincidence?" asked Sue . . .

Jessie climbed into Mrs. Sanders' car without protest and sat in the back seat, looking out. Remembering Eric's car and the way it was thrown down the bank, she trembled slightly and started to pant . . .

"I should keep her on a lead for a week at least,"

Sue told Mrs. Sanders. "She's had a nasty experience, you know."

"Of course I will. She's not the first dog I've had," snapped Mrs. Sanders, fastening her seat belt. "You can't tell me much about dogs, my girl."

When they reached Mrs. Sanders' neat, thirty-year-old bungalow, Jessie found everything ready for her—a bowl, with DOG written on it, a hook for her lead, a brush and comb and a towel to wipe her paws. There was a bean bag in the sitting room for her to lie on and a plastic basket for her in the neat modern kitchen. There were long windows which opened onto a small garden with a sand pit at the end which Mrs. Sanders called a "doggy toilet". The bungalow was on the edge of a town, but there were shops close by and a park where you could walk, with tennis courts, swings and a football field. Mrs. Sanders was seventy-two, though if you had asked her age she would have smiled charmingly and answered "Sixty-two". She had been sixty-two for ten years now, and her hair was completely white.

Jessie did not like living with Mrs. Sanders.

Everything ran to time in the bungalow: breakfast at eight-thirty, walks on a lead at nine, dinner at three, walks again in the evening. Then at last a run in the garden at about nine-thirty. The walks were very short. After living with Eric and Matt the days seemed very long to Jessie, who was now called Mabs. She missed Eric's cheerful voice, the trips in his car and the rides by bus to Trafalgar Square to rescue injured pigeons.

She tried to adapt: she wagged her tail at Mrs.

Sanders in the mornings and licked her hand when her dinner had been particularly delicious. But all the time she was thinking of Eric and hoping to return to him. She was happier than she had been in the kennels, but she was not truly happy, because at the back of her mind her need for Eric remained, and farther back still was the need for the boy who had found her as a pup—Matt. Mrs. Sanders could not replace either of them in Jessie's affection.

Matt and Eric were interchangeable: either would do, but however hard Jessie tried, they stood between her and Mrs. Sanders. And Mrs. Sanders recognized this and was angry. She hated it when Jessie sat by the back door hour after hour as though expecting a visitor. She hated the way Jessie would suddenly seem to recognize someone in the park or the street and would start to strain at the lead and wag her tail until her whole behind was squirming, and then at the last moment realize her mistake and return to her usual quiet self, her tail down, her eyes expressionless: quiet and obedient but not happy. Mrs. Sanders wanted to be adored; but Jessie could only adore her two absent friends, for in her doggy mind Mrs. Sanders was simply holding her prisoner until either she escaped or they came for her.

Mrs. Sanders became angrier and angrier, until she was shouting, "come away from that door Mabs. Come away at once, do you hear?" Sometimes she was so angry she threw water over Jessie—usually cold, but on one occasion hot and soapy. And the angrier she became the more Jessie longed for Eric. "I do *everything* for you," Mrs. Sanders complained angrily, "and what do I get in return? Nothing! Just a wag now and again."

Several times Mrs. Sanders nearly returned Jessie to the kennels and asked for her money back; only pride stopped her and an intense hatred of failure. So weeks passed while Jessie waited her chance, for never for one moment did she stop thinking of Eric. Time and time again she thought she saw him, only to be disappointed, and each time Mrs. Sanders felt more hurt inside. Her spaniel had worshipped her so she knew how loving and faithful a dog can be, and Jessie was neither, merely polite and well behaved like a visitor who would soon be leaving.

Spring changed to summer. Mrs. Sanders only let Jessie off the lead in enclosed places. She had taught her to answer to her new name. Her spaniel had been called Marty and she had decided that all her future dogs' names should begin with M, so Mabs was short for Mabel. Jessie accepted it as she accepted everything, with a polite disdain.

Then in August Mrs. Sanders decided to visit her sister. She packed a picnic and set off at six in the morning, wearing a summer dress and sandals, her car recently serviced, with Jessie sitting in the back, looking out of the window, thinking her own thoughts which had nothing whatever to do with her mistress.

They travelled through Reading and took the road to Oxford. At twelve-thirty they picnicked close to a river and Jessie, sniffing the air, smelt watercress. She became restless after that, staring out of the window of the car with increased interest, remembering the smell, remembering Matt. Mrs. Sanders, drenched in talcum powder and perfume, smelt like thousands of other women. Her house, polished to perfection with scented polish, every bit of the kitchen wiped down with bleach or disinfectant, had no real smell either to a dog. It was like a page with nothing written on it: without interest.

Matt had his own smell, and so had Eric. Humans could not recognize it, but Jessie could, and the smell of watercress reminded her of Matt. She sat on the back seat of the car on a special rug with DOG embroidered on it, her ears pricked and her whole body tense with expectation.

So, at last, they reached their destination, a neat mock-Tudor house, with a monkey puzzle tree in the garden and a lawn so perfectly mown it looked false.

"Now, Mabs, you must behave yourself," said Mrs. Sanders, clipping a lead onto Jessie's collar.

They found Mrs. Sanders' sister Betty and her husband behind the house, on a small patio, sitting in white garden chairs and drinking coffee. They kissed Mrs. Sanders warmly on the cheek. "So this is Mabs; she looks all right, rather a beauty actually, pedigree I would say," announced Betty in a loud cheerful voice. "Yes, definitely pedigree, I would say. What a bit of luck." She knelt down in front of Jessie, saying, "Come on, Mabs, that's a good girl. Don't you like your Auntie Betty? There's a pretty girl . . ."

And Jessie looked away across the neat garden, smelling watercress in the distance, remembering a house, a large kitchen, a bedroom with Matt in it—her first home.

They ate lunch with Jessie tied to the garden seat

and a bowl of water beside her. Being tied to a seat humiliated Jessie. It was something she had never experienced before. She sat very still, panting in the hot sunlight, for there was not a cloud in the sky, not a breath of wind anywhere. It was the hottest day of the year so far . . .

"I'll shut the gate. Do let her run, Doris," said Betty later. "She must want to relieve herself, though don't let her do it on the lawn or Cecil will not be happy. Sometimes I think he's in love with the lawn, I really do."

So Jessie wandered round the garden while the two ladies collapsed into garden chairs and dozed peacefully. She used her nose and learned all sorts of things—that a cat had climbed the monkey puzzle tree in the small hours, that mice had run along the split oak fence, that a dog had lifted his leg on the far side of the gate post—and, while she read these things rather as you might read a book, though by smell instead of eyes, she never stopped looking for a way out. She knew from the smell of watercress she was near her first home.

The split oak fence was too high for Jessie to jump, and on the other side of the garden a neatly clipped privet hedge was too thick to slip through. Only the gate remained. One autumn day Matt had built a "show jumping course" for her in the garden. So she measured her distance, took off and, banking the top of the gate, was over and running down the road before the two ladies sat up with a start.

"Whatever was that?"

"It sounded like the gate," said Betty, while her

husband slept peacefully as he did every afternoon in the large double bed upstairs.

"Mabs, where are you?" cried Mrs. Sanders, struggling to her hot, aching feet, and scrabbling for her sandals which she had taken off to rest them. "Mabs, come here, will you? Come here at once. Do as I say—Mabs!" she cried.

But Jessie was already smelling the air, setting off at a loping trot towards the water meadows, only one thought in her neat black head—to find Matt and the pleasant house where she had spent her puppyhood. It was as though Mrs. Sanders had never happened, had ceased to exist. All she had to do now was to find Matt and everything would be all right.

The house was still there. Nothing had changed on the outside except that the lawn needed mowing, the hedge clipping and the dead heads taken off the roses. But Jessie did not notice such things and went straight to the back door. At this time Matt would just have returned from school, would be throwing down his bag and crying out to Jessie, "I'm back at last. Are you all right, Jessie? Where's your ball?" Saying words she understood while she gazed up at him, her eyes shining a welcome, her tail wagging. She scratched on the familiar back door and whined. She could not smell Matt, only a smell of new-made pastry. A tall fair-haired lady opened the door and stared at Jessie. "What do you want? You don't live here," she said, quite kindly.

Jessie pushed past her and ran through the sitting

room, then on up the familiar stairs to Matt's room. It was just the same—the same furniture, the same bed—but not the same, because Matt was not there and it did not smell of Matt any more.

She stood holding up one paw as she looked around the room. None of her things were there either, and a small fair-haired girl lying on Matt's bed, her blue eyes terrified, started to shout, "Mum. There's a dog here. A black one. What shall I do? Mum! Help! *Mum*!"

Jessie fled back down the stairs, knocking the fair-haired lady sideways as she ran. The back door was still open, the garden basking in the sun. The places where she had played with Matt were still there, but not the same because Matt was not there. Everything was there, yet different . . . She stopped for a minute to smell the air. And now she knew where she was going: she was going to London to find Eric!

Nine

"YOU had better ring the police," Betty said. "I'll wake Cecil."

"She must have jumped the gate, drat her," replied Mrs. Sanders. "I'll just look down the road." She did not walk far because of her aching feet. She called, "Mabs, Mabs, come here at once," in a shrill voice.

But Jessie was half a mile away by now and, even if she had heard, she would not have obeyed.

"Well, she was always too big for me. Next time I'll choose something small. She never took to me, if you know what I mean," said Mrs. Sanders after Cecil had rung the police. "Let's have a cup of tea, shall we?"

"Don't you want to look farther? I can get the car out," suggested Cecil.

"If you like. But I don't want to be a trouble, and she was never happy with me. She always wanted to run off somewhere, and now she's managed it," said Mrs. Sanders, remembering Jessie's vigil by the door, waiting for someone who never turned up. "We never took to one another, if you know what I mean," she repeated.

Jessie headed across country, panting in the heat.

She had nearly eighty miles to cover, and she was far from it. She had never walked farther than half a mile with Mrs. Sanders and this soon began to tell. The pads on her paws were soft too, and the fields were hard and parched, either high in crops or prickly with stubble.

Every so often Jessie stopped to smell the air to fix her sense of direction, her nose high, her small white patch glinting in the evening sun. Several people saw her and they all thought the same thing: "That dog knows where she's going!"

A man on a tractor got down to call to her. A girl on a horse thought she recognized her as belonging to a friend and called, "Cleo, come here. You bad girl, come here at once."

Jessie heeded none of them. Brave and defiant, she loped on through the gathering dusk, while storm clouds gathered overhead telling her that rain was coming. She reached a wood and waited, hungry and tired, her pads sore. The rain crashed through the trees, branches bent and split beneath the deluge, which soaked Jessie and darkened dusk into night. She found refuge under rhododendrons and lay there exhausted, not thinking, just waiting for strength to return to her aching limbs.

When dawn came rosy pink she set off again, until after several hours she reached the Thames, lined with picnickers, thick with boats. This was where she would leave Oxfordshire and cross into Berkshire. She had hardly swum before, yet she knew how to do it by instinct. Children in a playground watched her go down to the water's edge, hesitate, then walk up and down the bank choosing a place to go in. The farther bank looked a long way off. A boat rowed by eight men with another man steering went up the river; a barge passed down.

Jessie launched herself at last, striking out for the farther shore, her head just visible. She neared the bank just as a motor boat went by, its wash lifting her up and then casting her down again. One of the men on board called out, "Look at that dog. She's swimming the Thames!" Dragging herself up the farther bank, Jessie shook herself; then loped on towards London. After a time she followed the road, trotting along the hard shoulder, the trucks sending up fumes which drowned all other smells, the sun hot on her back. Her pads were bleeding now, but still she went on.

On and on. Once again her determined gait stopped anyone interfering, for all the people who saw her knew she was going home. She went the shortest way, straight through Slough crowded with shoppers, pushing her way through endless legs, brushing against shopping bags, her head towards London. Then at last out into air fresher in spite of the trucks thundering by, the roads gleaming wet from recent rain, the sun shining again and making the roadside verges sparkle. There were dry fields yellow with ragwort, where lean horses dug their teeth into sparse earth, pulling out the remnants of grass. There was a market garden and miles and miles of trim houses. There was an inn, its parking lot cluttered with cars, the air loud with voices. Jessie took no notice of it, though a woman there cried, "Look at that dog. All alone. She'll be killed. Catch her someone, for goodness' sake."

"She knows where she's going: she's all right," said a man with a beard.

The traffic grew heavier. The fumes sank deep into Jessie's lungs. Her pace was growing slower now; her body wanted food and water. Soon she would have to stop, but London still beckoned, for Eric's room was her lair, her home, the only safe place left. There was nowhere else. She went down a bank and found water in a ditch, but she still needed food. She was not a killer and had a gun dog's teeth, soft enough to carry game without damaging it. She knew nothing of hunting, for she had always had food provided, first her mother's milk, then by Matt, Eric, and more recently Mrs. Sanders, but she found sandwiches thrown from a car window and ate them.

By evening she had reached the outskirts of London and, needing rest, turned off the main road down a side street where there were houses, one after another; with neat gardens at the back, but nowhere for an exhausted dog to rest. So she turned back again and, with the marvellous instinct of a dog, went on towards Lasbrook Common. And now she looked quite different, like an exhausted dog struggling to reach home, travelling by instinct alone, her mind on one thing only—reaching home. Several times people barred her way, one young woman even squatting on the pavement to say, "Come here, little doggy. You look hungry. Come here." Jessie simply skirted round her on to the road, avoiding the cars by a combination of instinct and luck, and continued her journey.

Not once was she tempted to ask for food or water,

to sit and plead. Now that she had reached London she felt her only hope was to press on, even though her bleeding paws left smudges of red on the pavement, her inside screamed with hunger and her throat was dry and parched with thirst. The fact that when she last saw Eric he was being taken away in an ambulance did not affect her. As far as she was concerned Eric would be there waiting in his shabby cluttered room and would open the door to her, and then she would be home. And there she would rest, safe at last.

Her legs continued to work. Her strong heart pumped fresh blood into her veins and, as she drew nearer to Lasbrook Common, her pace quickened. From somewhere inside herself she found a hidden store of strength, until she was almost galloping down the last familiar streets to home. The street lights were on. All along the road residents were locking up, putting out milk bottles, calling out "Good-night" to one another, slamming car doors, putting the keys in their pockets. A few dogs were being given last walks on the common, while not far away a train was on its final journey that day, the driver thinking of home.

Home! Jessie was nearly there. She felt like a dog on its last leg returning home to die, the pads of her paws quite raw now, her claws broken, muscles aching, tendons strained, for she had travelled fifty miles that day and the fumes were still in her lungs and the dust on her coat. She did not look for the house; she knew it by instinct—the shabby steps, the area where the garbage cans lived, the door which needed painting. Eric's car was no longer in the street lowering the "tone" of the neighborhood. The residents above were now putting out their lights and going to bed, oblivious of the black dog slipping down the steps, standing by the basement door whining, before she put up a bloodstained paw to scratch at the door and ask to be let in.

Jessie whined and scratched the door again and again, and then barked hoarsely. No one came to the door. Everything was in darkness now except for the rays of light cast by the street light above. She waited, then presently she lay exhausted against the door, certain that Eric would be there soon: that she only had to stay and he would arrive and let her in. So she pushed her nose against the door and slept on the hard stone doorstep, her body hunched with a sudden coldness.

A grey morning came. Jessie was so stiff she could hardly move, and there was still no sign of Eric. Only the two girls from the second floor flat tipping refuse into their garbage can stood looking at her. They were quite young. "She's the dog that awful man owned. What shall we do?" asked the taller, who had legs as thin as bean poles and hair the color of ripe corn.

"Fetch her some milk. Then phone the police," said her friend. So they returned to their flat and found the number of the nearest police station. The tall girl brought Jessie milk while the other talked to the police, and now the sun was shining over the millions of roof tops, reaching the basement with a single golden bar. Jessie drank the milk, watching the girl out of the corner of one eye. "The police are on their way," said the other girl, plumper, calmer, with dark hair and perfect teeth. "They'll take her to the kennels . . . But they may put her down."

"*We* can't have her," said the slim one firmly. "Come

on, or we'll be late for college. You're too soft-hearted, Denise. We've done our best. It's her owner's fault. He shouldn't have deserted her . . . Men are all the same, if you ask me."

"Not all of them," answered Denise. The sunshine lit up their glossy hair. They were dressed in the latest fashion, pink and purple, their faces made up.

Soon Jessie heard the police car. She stood up and made for the steps. She could recognize different engine sounds: if Eric had driven down the road in his old banger she would have known at once. She recognized the uniforms too; men dressed in them had taken Eric away from her, had delivered her to kennels and ultimately to Mrs. Sanders. Such men were to be feared, so she made herself very small as she went up the steps. Two policemen were getting out of their car now and she could see their black boots above her as she neared the top of the steps. She slunk round the corner, hoping to be invisible. If there had been grass or undergrowth she would have been, but not in a street in London. They turned at once and called to her. They ran after her down the street, but she ran faster. The grass was still damp on the common when she reached it. The police knew her name. "Jessie. Come on, Jess. Come on here; there's a good girl," they called. "Good doggie."

They were pretending to be Eric, but they were not Eric. Jessie knew that and ignored their calls. Then the police called to a woman walking across the common. "Please stop that dog, madam. She's a stray." But she was a dog lover and called back, "Why? What has she done wrong? She looks pedigree to me."

Jessie slipped through a deserted garden. Below lay the railway line. There were brambles on its banks, and sometimes rabbits. It was one of the wild parts of London which grow fewer every year. Jessie stopped and lay down. Instinct told her to stay there until dusk. The milk had quenched her thirst. Soon Eric would be back; then she would be safe. She was content to wait.

But Eric still lay in the hospital, his hair slowly growing on his shaven head. One leg was suspended in the air. He wanted to tell someone about Jessie, but however hard he tried he could not talk, nor could he write. When at last he managed the single word "Jess", the red-haired nurse who was near by said, "Not to worry. She's all right. She's waiting for you, I expect," imagining a woman somewhere. Stroking his hand she added kindly, "You'll be better soon, but not if you get excited." And when Eric tried to say some more she threatened him with: "If you don't calm down, we'll have to sedate you. You heard what the doctor said . . . No excitement, because we can't have you hemorrhaging again."

So, although he worried about Jessie and could remember nothing about the accident, Eric could not ask about her. It was like being gagged. Often when no nurse was around he would practice talking, but although he *thought* the words they did not emerge from his lips, and it was a frustrating and terrifying experience. And at the back of the mind there was always the thought, supposing I can never speak again? What if Matt returns and wants Jessie?

Meanwhile far away in Florida Matt wrote to Anne, telling her that he had had no news of Jessie, but that Florida was terrific. *"By the time I return home I shall be a champion swimmer,"* he wrote. *"We are hoping to settle in Suffolk eventually, where houses are still cheap. Then Jessie will be with us till she dies."*

When he visited New York he sent Uncle Eric a picture card of the Empire State Building, writing on the other side, *"New York is fabulous, but I can't wait to see Jessie again. Look after her and give her a bar of doggy chocolate from me. I promise I will pay you back when next we meet. Love, Matt."*

Ten

EVENING came with a rush of extra trains and Jessie knew it was time for Eric to return home. When he had left her alone in the flat, which was rarely, he had always returned at dusk, laughing as he entered his room, crying as often as not, "Come on, Jessie, there's just time for a run before dark."

They had gone out on the common together, down to the brook and back, stopping only to play ball on the mown piece; then chased each other round the swings, before going home for dinner.

She stood up now, stiff all over, every muscle screaming with pain, her stomach crying with hunger. She went to the brook first and drank. Men in suits were walking home across the common, small children were fighting over the swings. Any minute now and the street lights would be coming on. Autumn was in the air already, the leaves on the trees changing color.

Painfully Jessie went down the steps to the basement door, scratching at it, whining deep in her throat, pleading to be let in. If she had been a human being she might have knelt at the scratched and battered door, praying for Eric to appear, for a miracle to happen. But dogs' gods are human, and Eric was Jessie's god at this moment. He did not open the door, and there was no one to tell her that he was far away, thinking of her but incapable of speech. There was no one to tell her anything, no one now who cared for her except Matt, and Matt was thousands of miles away, imagining her with Eric.

Eventually she returned to the lair she had made for herself among some blackthorn bushes above the railway line. There she was hidden and the sun and the wind could not reach her.

There she stayed every day, returning to the basement each evening at the same time. She drank at the brook and often scavenged in the garbage cans for unwanted food, scattering lids and bits of paper over the area to the fury of the residents, who informed the Royal Society for the Prevention of Cruelty to Animals and the local Town Council.

"It's a disgrace," they said. "This place is beginning to look like a dump. If you don't do something we'll demand a reduction in the rates. No, we can't catch her. It's not our job anyway."

One evening in September, Jessie found the road blocked by a Council official, an RSPCA Inspector and two policemen. Food was waiting for her by Eric's door. They were all standing quietly out of sight, or so they thought, and as she came across the common the message went out, "She's on her way. Dead on time, just like the residents said—between six and six-thirty."

The men were all kind and jovial, anxious to catch the poor dog for her own good, thinking she would be better off in the kennels or humanely put to sleep than pining for a master who was gone . . . But Jessie did not know this. As she crossed the common and reached the road, she smelt something unusual. She stopped and stood, holding up a paw. What she smelt was excitement, which smells akin to fear. And fear means danger, so now there was danger lurking in the street where Eric lived and, what was worse, danger in uniform. This meant two things to Jessie, for the uniforms might be there to take Eric away again or to catch her, and she could not tell which.

The men saw her and froze, standing as still as statues. But Jessie could smell them better than a human being might see them. She knew where each one stood. She could smell the food in the area by Eric's door as well and it made her saliva run, but still she turned away. She went back across the common and through the overgrown garden, and sat waiting above the railway line for them to go, which might take hours or days, but had to be endured.

But they did not go. "She smelt us," said the Inspector.

"She's gone to that rough land by the railway," said one of the policemen.

"We had better follow her," said the man from the council, so they started to run across the common.

"It will be dark soon," said the Inspector, puffing.

The man from the council knew the overgrown garden well, because the council wanted to buy it for new houses, except that the owner would not sell. "If only the dog was white," he said, getting left behind because he spent most of his life in his office or his car, "or brown and white—anything but black we'd soon see her."

104

The policemen were the fittest, and soon saw Jessie. Because the wind was in the wrong direction, Jessie did not smell them at once, but still sat staring at the railway line. They waved their arms and then one cried hoarsely, "She's by the line. She'll never cross it." But Jessie turned and saw them and started to run along the side of the track.

"She'll never cross it," repeated the policeman.

The side of the line was strewn with broken bottles, beer cans and sweet papers. A broken bottle sliced Jessie's foreleg as she ran, leaving a gash half an inch deep, but she hardly felt the pain nor the bright red blood dripping down her leg.

"She can't get on the line; it's fenced all the way. It has to be," said the man from the council.

But Jessie found a way through where foxes had dug under the wire, and slipped through unseen. Now in the gathering dusk the men lost sight of her; one minute she was there, the next she was gone, slipping down the bank, crossing the line and avoiding the rails, somehow knowing they were dangerous, that even to touch them might mean instant death.

"If she's crossed the line she may have been electrocuted, and that will solve our problem," said the man from the council, wiping sweat from a pudgy face with eyes set deep, a face which had earned him the name of "piggy" among his enemies.

"You can't say that," replied the Inspector, whose job was to protect animals from cruelty.

Jessie loped away from the line, across the wasteland which so often stands on the outskirts of cities, towards a distant wood. Her injured leg was leaving a trail of blood, but instinct told her that when she reached the wood she would be safe. Darkness was like a shield around her. There was no noise behind her now because her pursuers had turned back, filled with a sense of failure.

"Perhaps she will keep away now. Perhaps she's got the message," said the man from the council, sick of angry telephone calls.

"Pity she wasn't electrocuted; it would have been a quick death," said the tallest of the policemen, who loved cats but did not care for dogs. "We can't have her fouling the pavements; it's against the law."

As if we didn't know! thought the man from the council, who kept no animals himself, not even a budgerigar. "And it's not just the fouling of the pavements; it's the contents of garbage cans strewn everywhere. It's a health hazard in more ways than one. And she could cause an accident," he added, his feet aching.

"I'll put a trap out for her," promised the Inspector. "Not to worry," he said. "I've never failed yet with a trap."

Jessie crawled into the wood and lay down. She could feel a searing pain in her injured foreleg, but there were no more footsteps in pursuit. It was a small grubby wood, the sort you see on the edge of towns where thoughtless people dump rubbish, and town foxes have their earths and live in comparative peace, with rats, the odd weasel or stoat and a variety of birds which nest in the stunted trees. It was thick with nettles and a wild tangle of weeds and blackberry bushes. The sun never really reached to the bottom of the wood, but in a clearing children had erected a makeshift swing and built themselves a hut out of branches and dead wood. It was here beneath the branches Jessie eventually lay down exhausted, her paw throbbing, her mind in turmoil, with no thought in it except to find Eric, for the worse life became the more pressing was her need of him.

She was awakened by a feeling of warmth next to her and a strange feeling of contentment. The sun was shining wanly through the branches above her, and a dog was whining and licking her cut leg.

Half-lurcher, half-Doberman, the local children called him the "Hound of the Baskervilles" after a story about Sherlock Holmes. After being dumped on the motorway by a family who had called him Tinker and loved him as a puppy, but grown tired of him later; who had thought that to dump him would at least give him a chance (never considering how it might feel to him to be abandoned), Tinker had adjusted quickly to a life in the wild. Now he coaxed Jessie to her feet and persuaded her to follow him to his lair, which lay in the deepest part of the wood, surrounded by blackthorn, hawthorn and brambles. There she found a half-eaten rabbit which she devoured instantly. After that she slept, and wakened with an overpowering thirst. She limped through the wood after Tinker to a stagnant pond where she drank before returning to his lair, and there she lay for nearly a week. Tinker stayed with her, departing only to find food for them both—rabbits, voles, once even a chicken, on which they feasted. Then one moonlit night they mated in a clearing, watched only by the birds in the trees above them.

It was winter now. Days grew shorter, nights longer. After seven days, when Jessie's leg was less painful, the urge to find Eric came over her again. Tinker went with her as far as the railway line; then watched her cross over, a deep whine in his throat because he was afraid to follow. Near the hole in the mesh the Inspector had set a wooden trap with half a chicken inside, but Jessie took one look and passed on, trotting through the deserted garden and on across the common in the twilight. It was growing dark and the lights were coming on along the street. Eric's car was not there, and the garbage cans had been emptied recently. Jessie slipped down the steps and stood by the familiar door, giving short, sharp barks. It was late and she thought that Eric might be asleep, for he had always been one for sleeping, so that time and time again Jessie had had to wake him at dinner time.

But this time no one came to open the door. Only the girls on the second floor looked out of a window and called to one another, "It's that dog again. She's back. What shall we do?"

Nothing smelt of Eric any more. Instead the whole place smelt of garbage cans, damp and deserted, for Eric had paid a year's rent in advance, so no one could move his belongings or wash the dirty crocks which cluttered the sink green with mold. The walls were so damp that fungi had started to grow on them, and Jessie's bed was damp and smelly. And although Jessie could see none of it, she knew it by the smell from beneath the door. Hearing the girls, she left the door and, climbing the steps, limped away, tail down, dragging one leg after another.

Now days followed which slowly turned into weeks. Jessie only occasionally went in search of Eric now. Soon her coat had no shine on it and, though Tinker took her hunting and taught her to kill, she was now so riddled with worms and infested with lice that, however much she ate, she seemed to be growing thinner all the time. Tinker killed everything he could find. He raided gardens while Jessie stood nervously outside, returning with guinea pigs, chickens, once even a gerbil. And so the two dogs became enemies to the local children, who hunted them without mercy, throwing stones at them and shooting them with catapults. Enraged fathers chased them with guns; youths on motorbikes pursued them at relentless speed. Tinker's haunches were peppered with air gun pellets. Jessie was hit by a stone which left her partially deaf in one ear. She grew increasingly nervous until the slightest rustle would frighten her. Heavy in pup, she no longer looked pedigree. Her ribs stood out and even her neck had grown thin. And the thinner and more disreputable she and Tinker became, the more the children hunted them.

The weather grew colder and rain fell for days on end. Now Jessie was so weak she rarely had the strength to go in search of Eric. Her leg had not healed and was now permanently infected, and she had a hacking cough. Tinker, being a stronger dog, suffered less. His lurcher mother had come from a long strain of gypsy dogs, so he could stand the weather, the lice and the worms better than Jessie, and he was not in pup.

Often now he went hunting alone, bringing back anything he could find to share with Jessie, while she slept more and more, her eyes slowly becoming oozy with pus, her ears cankerous, her bedraggled coat falling out in patches. Her infected leg became worse as her general health deteriorated, until everything seemed to be dragging her down. Often she dreamed of Eric, sometimes of Matt. She dug deeper into the earth for warmth, curled herself tighter, covering her nose with her tail.

Then everything froze, water turned to thick ice; only the brook on the common continued to run. When evening came Jessie and Tinker set off for the common. Jessie moved very slowly now, a shadow of her former self, just days away from death. But they both knew they had to drink if they were to survive. A big courageous dog, who could fight his way out of any scrap, Tinker went ahead. He had never crossed the railway line before, but thirst was stronger than fear. He looked back at Jessie and then went on down the bank. He could hear a train approaching, but there was time to get across the line. He did not hear Jessie's quick bark of warning, but hurried on, oblivious of the danger from the live rail which became lethal as a train approached. Another second and one of his large tan forepaws had touched the rail and he was dead; stretched out across the line, a huge hulk of a dog, amber-eyed, brown-ruffed, quite dead.

Jessie waited, one paw in the air, until the train had passed. She stopped to look at the remains of her friend. Instinct told her that he was dead, and she dared not touch what was left of him. Thirst drove her on alone through the mesh hole in the fence, through the deserted garden to the familiar common, and after she quenched her thirst at the brook, fear drove her back to the wood. It was one of the coldest nights in years; every branch, every leaf, every blade of grass was white with frost. Taps froze in houses, water in car radiators. Nothing seemed to move. It was as though the whole world was frozen. Jessie curled herself into a tighter ball, trying to shut out the world, while overhead a plane droned coming in to land.

She did not move again for hours. She knew she was dying and the pups she carried would die with her. She did not fear death; all she wanted was one last chance to find Eric: if she could achieve that she would die happy.

Eleven

ANNE had written inviting Matt to stay. Now there was a second letter in a strange handwriting sent to his father's office. His father gave it to him at dinner. "I nearly opened it, but then I thought you would rather do it yourself," he said.

"It's from England," said Matt's mother.

"From Uncle Eric perhaps?" suggested Matt, looking at the stamps.

"No, it isn't his writing."

Matt tore the envelope open. Inside the letter was brief and to the point. Turning pale, he handed it to his mother. "It isn't true, is it? It's a joke, isn't it?" he shouted. "It isn't from Uncle Eric, is it? It isn't true, is it? There's been a mix-up."

Matt's mother read it out loud, her voice breaking towards the end.

" 'Dear Matt, I am writing this for your Uncle, who had a bad car accident last winter. He has been unconscious and in a coma, but now he can talk a little he wants me to tell you that he understands that Jessie was taken away by the police and placed in the kennels. He suggests contacting the Kent police for further

112

details. He wants me to say how sorry he is and sends his love.' And it's signed, *'Joan Singer, Staff Nurse,'* " Matt's mother finished.

"It isn't true, is it?" repeated Matt, pushing his dinner away.

"Yes, it must be. Poor Eric. He's in a hospital, in Kent. It happened last winter," said Matt's mother. "And now it's winter in England again. Why didn't anyone *tell* us?"

"Because your brother never had our address over here," said Matt's father.

"Yes, he did, because I wrote to him," Matt answered. "What are we going to do?"

"Ring the hospital and the Kent police. What's the time in England?" cried Matt's mother, standing up.

"It doesn't matter. Both stay open all night. You stay here with me, Matt," said his father.

"Why?"

"Because I say so."

"Yes, stay. Eat your dinner. Don't worry. Everything may be all right," said his mother, leaving the room.

"I want Jessie. I want her back. She's mine," Matt said.

It was some time before his mother returned, and then she looked shaken. "Eric's still very ill. I shall have to go to England. He's got no one else. I must go," she cried, looking from one to the other of them.

"What about Jessie? Where is she? What's happened to her?" shouted Matt.

113

"The police say she's been found a home. They took her to the kennels and they say she wasn't hurt in the accident."

"Does that mean I can't have her back?" asked Matt, his voice suddenly flat and hopeless.

"I'm afraid so. They waited the customary time and no one came forward, so they were within the law. And the kennels aren't likely to disclose the home," replied his mother.

Tears streamed down Matt's face. "But she may not be happy. She may want Uncle Eric or me."

"She'll be all right," his father said. "Dogs soon adapt. The police are right: if she's been given away, she's been given away. There's nothing we can do about it."

"But she's still *mine*. She's never stopped being mine. She can't just be taken away like that," shouted Matt. "It isn't fair. Can't you see that? I never *gave* her to Uncle Eric."

"The police weren't to know that, were they?" said his father.

Matt's mother looked out of the window; there was not a cloud in the sky. She dared not tell Matt that the police had said that Jessie had waited all day and night with Eric, nor how she had stood on the verge barking for help. If she told him he would crack; he would imagine the scene and never get over it. So she had to pretend that Jessie had simply been taken away by the police, that everything had happened quickly with no long night of waiting in between.

"I'll book a flight now. After all, we were going next month anyway," she said, hurrying from the room.

"I'm going with you. Term's ending tomorrow. I'm not staying behind," Matt called after her.

Matt's father nodded. "I'll be all right on my own. Matt will be company for you, love," he called.

"I'll start packing then," Matt said, running towards his bedroom.

"Pack all your warm clothes," his mother called, a telephone directory in her hand. "It'll be winter in England. Poor Eric, I keep thinking of him lying in the hospital all that time alone, without any visitors, or flowers, or anything. I feel so guilty," she said before dialling a number. "We had better fly to New York and then on to England."

"Or get a flight straight from Miami," said Matt's father. "That's the best way, love; there's sure to be a flight."

Matt threw clothes into a suitcase and then sat on it. His heart would not stop pounding and his mouth felt dry. He was seeing the crash all the time now, a pile-up of cars and Uncle Eric lying in the road. And Jessie, where was Jessie? Oh God, Jessie . . . Was it true that he would never see her again? She was still his. He had never given her away to anyone. It was not his fault he had had to go to America. God knows he had not wanted to go. He had met many dogs recently, but none could hold a candle to Jessie, and now she was gone. Putting a strap round his case, he swallowed the tears which were threatening to stream down his face. And what about Uncle Eric? Mad Uncle Eric with his scarecrows, whom no one took seriously, who was a bit of a joke really, who was now lying unable to write a letter. It was too awful to think about, but it would not go away. It had happened, whether Matt liked it or not, and it could not be changed.

The plane left on time. The journey seemed endless. Matt and his mother hardly talked. Matt was thinking only of Jessie, while his mother was remembering Eric, wondering how she would find him when they reached England. Would he ever walk again for instance? Or talk for that matter? There was so much she should have asked and hadn't when she rang the hospital. Now she felt quite numb and afraid.

Heathrow was grey and wet when they reached it. They took an underground train to Victoria. Too tired to talk, they sat bemused by the different climate and the change of time. People appeared to be going to work. Victoria Station was crowded and it was raining.

"God! How I hate hospitals," Matt's mother said, suddenly looking as grey as the wet pavement beneath their feet.

"Shouldn't we take something—flowers or something?" asked Matt.

"Eric hated picking flowers. He always said they should be left in peace. He thought picking flowers was like killing a spider—unforgivable," she said, smiling in spite of herself.

"What's happened to his scarecrows?" asked Matt when they were sitting on the train to Kent.

"God knows . . ."

"Why do you talk about him in the past?"

"It was unintentional."

"You think he's going to die, don't you?"

"No. The accident was on February 28. It's a long time ago, and if he was going to die he would have died then. That's why you can't expect to have Jessie back. It wouldn't be fair, would it? Not after ten months. It's as long as *we* had her, isn't it?"

"I don't want to talk about it," Matt answered looking out of the train window, not seeing the houses and back garden outside but Jessie as a pup welcoming him home from school.

"Dogs are all the same really. We'll get you another puppy as soon as we are properly settled in East Anglia," his mother told him.

"I don't think I want one. I only want Jessie," he said.

"Don't be a baby, Matt."

"I wish the train would hurry up. Why does time pass so slowly when you're anxious and so fast when you're happy?" asked Matt.

"I don't know. But it's the next station now, so get your things together," his mother said.

It seemed a long way from Florida. Everything looked smaller and older, even the people sitting opposite them. They bought Eric newspapers and chocolates before hailing a taxi. It was still raining from a leaden sky.

"Do you think Uncle Eric will remember the crash?"

"I don't think so." His mother's teeth were chattering when they reached the hospital and inquired after Eric. A nurse told them to sit down. "A doctor's just doing his rounds," she said.

"How is Mr. Morgan doing?" asked Matt's mother.

"Progressing."

"Be prepared for a shock, Matt," his mother said. "And don't ask a lot of questions. Remember, he's still very ill."

Matt would never forget the next half hour, the long ward, the sick men, the polished floor, Uncle Eric lying in bed sadly changed, just able to raise a hand in greeting, his hair shaved off so that he looked like a convict, his mouth crooked, his eyes without their sparkle. Everything he did seemed to be in slow motion, so that they had to wait on every word which came slowly and only with intense effort. Quite soon Matt's mother told Matt to go back to Reception and sit there. Uncle Eric raised his hand slowly in farewell. A nurse smiled at Matt, but he was still in a state of shock. If that's what can happen to you driving a car then I'm never going to drive, he thought, walking towards Reception.

And he had not mentioned Jessie. Somehow she seemed to matter less when compared with Uncle Eric's afflictions. Matt read the comics in Reception, but the words never reached his brain, for he kept seeing Jessie scared and hurt being dragged away to the kennels.

Presently his mother joined him. "I've spoken to Staff Nurse and tomorrow I shall see the doctor. Apparently he's making good progress. They are very pleased with him," she told Matt, her eyes awash with tears. "Truly, Matt, truly," she added with a choke in her voice. "So don't be too cast down."

"Did you manage to talk to him?" asked Matt. "Did

you ask about Jessie?"

"A little, but it distresses him to talk about her. But I've got his apartment key. We're going straight there to pick up his mail and clean up a bit, because the lease runs out on January 1st."

"Isn't he going back there?" asked Matt, following her out of the hospital.

"No. He's going to be in a wheelchair for a bit and he may never be able to drive again, but I don't think he wants to anyway. Come on, let's catch a bus to the station."

Already she was making the best of a bad job, coming to terms with it. She had always been like that, thought Matt. Every new move, every stormy row with his father; she had always come to terms with it within twenty-four hours. But things had been easier lately. Some time in America, she had talked to Matt's father, telling him that he must consider Matt as well as himself. He had changed, becoming kinder and more generous, and the rows were fewer.

"Where are we going then? I mean, where exactly is Uncle Eric's flat, apartment, whatever you call it?" Matt asked, following his mother on to a bus.

"By Lasbrook Common. We go to Hammersmith and then change. It will take hours, but never mind," she said looking at her watch, which was still set at Miami time.

"When will we ring Dad?" asked Matt.

"This evening."

"Won't it be too late?"

"He said he didn't mind," she answered.

Later they caught an underground train from

119

Victoria, then changed onto another train. Matt was very tired now. The long journey, the shock of seeing his sick uncle, the loss of Jessie, all helped to depress him. His mother was tired too and had ceased looking around her, just seemed to be dozing, or putting one foot in front of another in a kind of dream.

"We'll stay in a hotel tonight," she said when at last they reached open air again. "Mind how you cross the road. Remember that the traffic goes the other way. We don't want *you* in the hospital too." She was trying to smile, and failing. Her summer dress was creased and too light for a winter's day. Over it she wore a newly acquired fur coat, while Matt was in jeans, a sweat shirt and a yellow zip-up jacket. All around them were houses now, street after street of them; they found a crossing more by instinct than anything else. The trees along the streets were bereft of leaves. Cars passed incessantly. "His house is No. 10 Lasbrook Road, opposite the common, and his apartment is Flat B," said Matt's mother.

"It all sounds so complicated," grumbled Matt.

"We should have bought an A to Z map," she said.

They found the common at last, stretching away into the distance. Children were kicking a ball on it and a mother was pushing a stroller with a squalling baby inside, while in the distance ducks flapped their wings. Matt imagined Jessie running across the grass. Tears flooded his eyes. All this way for nothing, he thought. Why did it have to happen? Why can't she be here with Uncle Eric? Both waiting for us!

"Here it is, No. 10," said his mother, looking up at a tall house. "Flat B: where is it?"

"B is for basement and it's down there. There's an arrow," said Matt grimly. "Look—down those steps by the garbage cans." They went down the steps. The cans needed emptying. The walls were damp. A panic-stricken mouse ran between their feet. They looked through a window and saw the chaos inside.

"It's terrible. How *could* you let him live here? It's a slum. Why didn't you help him? Dad earns enough. Why didn't you send him money? We could have sent him money for Jessie," shouted Matt.

Ignoring him, his mother unlocked the door and peered in.

Jessie's bed was still in a corner. The sink was still full of dirty crocks waiting to be washed up. There was a mouse on Eric's bed which sat looking at them beady-eyed. There were crumbs on the carpet along with mouse droppings. There was one poor scarecrow left with hair made of string. He leaned against a chair, sagging like an old man too thin for his clothes. Matt and his mother stood and stared in dismay, tears running down their faces.

"I didn't know," said Matt's mother at last. "He never told us he was short of money."

Twelve

"THERE'S not even a proper bathroom, and the kitchen's disgusting," cried Matt, not looking at Jessie's basket.

"Can we help?" Denise and her friend Linda from the second floor flat darkened the doorway. "Are you looking for Mr. Morgan? He had an accident. He hasn't been seen for months," said Denise.

"I'm his sister. We were in America. We didn't know," announced Matt's mother, holding out her hand.

They looked at her in surprise. "We didn't think he had any relations," said Linda. "The police called and asked some questions, but we couldn't help."

Matt's mother was picking up a pile of letters off the mat now. Several were in brown envelopes and addressed in red. "The water board switched the water off last week, and the electricity people cut that off, oh, months back. Mr. Birch the landlord let them in," said Denise.

"I quite understand. My brother had a terrible accident. He's only just out of a coma and can't talk properly yet—smashed skull, smashed pelvis, the lot really, and it wasn't his fault; the police told me that." Matt looked at his mother and saw how tense she was, as tense as a bit of wire stretched tight. There were lines round her eyes and she had not made up her face for hours.

"He had a dog, a sweet little thing," Linda said, pushing hair out of hazel eyes. "She kept coming back. We called the council half a dozen times and the RSPCA. Didn't we, Denise?"

"That's right. They all came here one day—a council man, an RSPCA Inspector, police, the lot. But they couldn't catch her . . ."

"When was that?" asked Matt, his body fired with sudden hope.

"Oh, months ago. Back in the summer. I should think she's dead by now, poor little thing," said Linda. "We put out milk for her. We did our best, but after she was chased she was so nervous you couldn't get near her; it was pathetic."

Matt saw Jessie chased. He saw her starving. He saw her looking for Eric, waiting. It was too unbearable to think about.

"She was sent to the kennels. I checked that with the police. She was found a new home, miles away," said Matt's mother, looking at Matt's small tense face, seeing the sudden hope which was there. "So it must have been another dog," she added.

"It wasn't. It was the same dog waiting to be let in, barking and barking. Oh God, it was awful and I feel so guilty. We should have done more . . . I know we should, but we had our exams; you know how it is . . . And we were so busy rushing here and there and we thought it was the council's job to deal with, not ours. I mean, what do people pay taxes for?" asked Denise, her voice breaking.

"When was she last here?" asked Matt in a small tight voice, tight because he was afraid he would start choking in a moment, might even be sick, or faint—he felt so ill with hope.

"A month, I suppose," said Linda, looking at Denise for confirmation.

"Yes, about a month ago, and she looked terrible. I don't think she can still be alive. I don't really; better dead, I think; a happy release really," said Denise, looking into Matt's miserable face. "Really, honestly, she could hardly walk. We wanted to catch her, but we were on our way out. We had a taxi waiting. It was one of *those* evenings and freezing cold too. I'm sure she isn't still alive."

"She was *my* dog," Matt said, looking at the two girls. "She was never Uncle Eric's. He was just looking after her for me . . ."

"He was a funny sort, but he looked after her as best he could and treated her like a child," Linda told him. "They loved each other; there was no doubt about that."

"None at all," agreed Denise.

"She used to come across the common. They say she lived above the railway line; that's what the police said. They did try to catch her several times. It was nobody's fault; just one of those things. Would you like to come upstairs for a cup of tea? You look famished and it's getting colder every minute," said Denise, pulling a sweater tighter round her shoulders.

"That's very kind of you. Thank you very much. It's a long time since I've tasted a cup of real English tea," said Matt's mother.

"I'm going across the common to the railway line, just to look. I won't be long," Matt said.

"It'll be dark soon and we haven't had anything to eat all day. Don't be long, Matt, do you hear? Don't be long."

Matt hardly heard his mother because what the girls had said seemed to be going round and round in his head now at the speed of an express train. A low mist hung over the common. The grass was wet. In the surrounding houses the lights were already on. None of it registered with Matt. He could have been walking on the moon, or across a desert, for all he saw of his surroundings. And now he was away from the others he could cry unashamedly, the tears splashing down his suntanned face like a sudden rain storm.

He heard a train and went towards it, through the deserted garden which now had a FOR SALE notice by the entrance. Another minute and he was standing above the line staring down at the tracks . . . Beyond was rough land where a few thin horses grazed, and beyond that a wood. He watched three trains go by, crammed now with workers all leading their separate lives: like ants, he thought, returning to their anthill. How many had seen Jessie, he wondered? And how had she reached London after being found a new home? Probably he would never know. Her life after the crash would remain a mystery and she would never have a neat grave now with her name on a stone, but lie where she had fallen, her bones picked clean by carnivorous birds and rats.

Afterwards he could never say what made him call

her name. Not once but over and over again, "Jessie, Jess, Jess, Jessie, where are you?" Really it was more a lament than a call, for it held a wailing note of despair. "Jessie, Jessie, Jess, Jess. Please come, Jessie. Jessie." He almost added, "I can't live without you," but knew it was not true, that he would go on in spite of her loss, because he had to. He sat down for a minute because suddenly the sky seemed to be moving, the very earth rocking. Another minute standing and he would have fainted. He thought he heard his mother calling, "Matt, come back. Matt. Where are you? I'm waiting." But he wasn't sure, for now he wasn't sure of anything any more. He put his head in his hands and cried, tired and unashamed above the line, far from home, any home.

Deep in the woods Jessie heard him and whined uneasily. The voice brought back the past. He was not Eric, but he had been there before Eric, and she had trusted him. Wearily she struggled to her feet, her whole body aching, her breath coming in gasps. He was calling and she had to go; however hard, however painful, his call had always been something she had obeyed and this time it was no different. She had to go . . .

She went on three legs, her body heavy with puppies, her eyes gummed with pus, her tail down. Across the wasteland she went, down to the line, dragging one leg after the other. Matt was just about to leave when he saw her carrying her tired body on three legs, her head lifted in hope, smelling for him, because she could not see. For a moment he thought she was a ghost. Then he was calling, "Jessie, I'm here. Be careful, Jessie," and now in the distance he could hear a train and he called, "Wait, Jessie . . . Wait . . . Wait . . . Don't move," and now the train was within their sight, lit up and hurtling through the dusk . . . He shut his eyes and screamed, "Wait, Jessie, wait!" and could not bear to open them again for fear of what he might see . . .

Then he heard her whine, and now she was dragging herself towards him, her ears flat against her head, her tail moving faintly in a guilty uncertain way. He knelt on the damp ground crying, "Jessie, Jessie. Oh, my poor Jessie!" and he knelt there so long cradling her head in his arms that his mother appeared looking for him. Then he raised a tear-stained face and cried, "She's dying. She's come home to die. Mum, we're too late."

"Are you sure it's Jessie? She doesn't look the same," his mother said, standing like a lost soul in her fur coat.

Matt raised Jessie's head and, pointing to the white on her chin, said, "It *is* Jessie. She heard my voice. Do something, Mum . . ."

His mother found a man walking alone on the common and brought him to help. He had longish fair hair and grey eyes. "I can't carry her, and Matt isn't strong enough. Can you help? She's dying," she said, and her voice was thick with unshed tears.

The man bent down and picked up Jessie in one quick movement. "She's ill and crawling with vermin," he said in concern, walking ahead of them across the common to where Denise and Linda were waiting, the lights from their rooms shining out on the pavement.

"She's only just alive," said the man, eyeing the two girls. "She's hardly any pulse. And just listen to her breathing . . ."

"Bring her upstairs," Denise said. "At least it's warm."

The man laid Jessie gently down on a blanket Linda provided, and whenever the Labrador caught a glimpse of Matt her tail moved slowly in welcome.

"Best have her put down. Just look at that paw: it's twice its normal size. And she's in pup too by the look of it," said the man.

"I'm ringing a vet," Linda told Matt, leafing through a yellow directory. "I'm quite ready to pay."

"No, of course not, we'll pay," said Matt's mother, taking off her coat.

"Well, I'll go now. Good luck," said the man, and Matt shook his hand while his mother said, "I don't know how to thank you."

"Don't, then. I was happy to oblige," he said, smiling at the girls as he left.

They waited for the vet, and time seemed to stand still as they waited. The atmosphere was thick with anxiety and gloom, because every breath seemed to be Jessie's last.

It took the vet ten minutes to reach them, and he was young and quick and angry. "I've never seen anything so terrible in my whole life," he fumed, staring round the room. "You should all be prosecuted. She's a beautiful dog—or was . . ."

They tried to explain. But he would not listen. "I

thought we lived in a civilized country," he raved, staring at them belligerently through thick-lensed glasses. "It seems I was wrong."

"It wasn't our fault," said Denise.

"She ran away and came back in search of her owner, who was terribly injured in a road crash," said Matt's mother. "We've been in America and didn't know."

"That's right," said Matt. "We didn't know. Okay? We didn't know."

"Well, you're gong to have to have her put down; put out of her misery, poor thing," the vet said, reaching for his bag . . .

There was a second of utter, painful silence before Matt, who was holding Jessie's head in his hands, shouted, "No. I won't have it. She's mine and I won't have it done. I'm keeping her. You're not taking her away from me; no one is, not ever again."

The vet looked at Matt and remembering his own youth said, "You want me to try to save her then?" Matt nodded, his stricken face pleading, his eyes swollen with tears.

"We'll try then, but I dare not take her to the doctor's office; she's too ill," the vet told him.

"She can stay here," said Denise, quietly going to put the kettle on, reckoning that everyone would need a cup of tea before they were through.

"We'll give her a shot of penicillin first," said the vet, opening his case. "Then a vitamin injection. Then we'll put her on a drip. Okay?" he asked, looking at Matt.

"Okay." Matt was still holding Jessie's head in his

hands.

No one spoke again and all they could hear was Jessie's breathing in and out, sounding like a table being dragged across a stone floor. "Oh God, let her live," prayed Matt inside his head. "Let her get better. Please, God. Just this once. It's all I ask."

"Keep her wrapped in the blanket, and stay with her all night," the vet said, looking at Matt. "Don't move the drip. I will be back in the morning. If she's dead before then, give me a ring. Here's my card if you're worried. Obviously she must stay where she is. If she gets through tonight she may survive; she's young and her heart is in good shape. Okay?"

"Okay," replied Matt and it was then that he decided that he really did want to be a vet when he was grown up.

"Call me if you're worried," added the vet as he left, and Matt thought: as if we aren't worried now!

"I'm so sorry to inflict ourselves on you like this. It's so embarrassing," said Matt's mother, turning to Denise.

"It's all right. You can have the spare room and Matt can have a sleeping bag, and we've got loads of eggs if you would like an omelette," Denise offered.

"Are you sure?"

"Absolutely."

"What about ringing Dad? Won't he be getting anxious?" asked Matt, looking at the drip's plastic bag, which was attached to a chair above Jessie's head and then by plastic tube to her uninjured front leg above her black paw—the one with the pink claws, only the pink claws were hardly visible now, having been worn away by constant use.

"Use our phone. You can find out how much the call costs and pay us afterwards," suggested Linda.

So they stayed the night. Matt wanted to remain awake, but sleep overcame him almost as soon as he lay down, and it was Linda and Denise who took it in turns to keep watch over Jessie, creeping into the sitting room at half-hour intervals throughout the winter night.

When Matt wakened in the morning he found Jessie's eyes were better already, and she was gazing at him, with love. Seeing he was awake, she wagged her tail as though to say, "We're together again, so everything is going to be all right," before letting her head flop back onto the blanket in tired relief. Her look brought Matt close to tears again as he adjusted the blanket so that it covered every part of her except her head and the paw attached to the drip. Then, drawing back the curtains, he looked out on a London morning so different from one in Florida. His mother appeared on tiptoe to whisper, "Is she all right? We can't stay here. It isn't fair to the girls, but we can't take Jessie to a hotel, so where can we go, Matt?"

"I'm not leaving her, not ever again," retorted Matt defiantly, looking small and vulnerable in his striped pajamas.

"The vet could have her until we are settled. She would be in good hands with him," suggested his mother tentatively.

"Can't you see it wouldn't work? It would break her

heart and stop her getting better. She would think we had deserted her again—can't you see?" cried Matt. "Are you thick or something?"

His mother sighed. "There's no need to be rude. It doesn't help. I'm going to get dressed; then I'm going to tidy Eric's room—it's in a terrible state," she said.

"What about his valuables? You can't leave them there," Matt said.

"There's nothing worth keeping. Just a few paperbacks and his address book. I'll put them in carrier bags; it's the best I can do. God, I'm tired," she said, going back to the spare room to dress. Later she returned with two carrier bags full of those of Eric's belongings worth saving, and then went out again to buy food for breakfast and a bottle of wine and some chocolates for Denise and Linda as a thank-you present.

The vet appeared, just as they were having a late breakfast all together in the sitting room. "My word, she's a tough little thing," he said, sliding the drip out of Jessie's paw with expert fingers. "She looks a hundred per cent better already."

"I think she's got nine lives," said Matt, smiling for the first time in days. "She was nearly drowned once—on purpose."

The vet smiled back, and after listening to Jessie's chest said, "Almost clear already. You can tell she hasn't had antibiotics before. They always work best the first time. I'll give you some penicillin tablets, and ointment for her eyes, and a spray for the lice; and she will need worming soon—when she's eating normally again—say, in a week. I'll give you something

132

safe for a bitch in whelp, because the pups *are* still alive and kicking," he added, listening to her stomach. "She'll need extra vitamins, of course."

"Pups are the last thing we want," Matt's mother said, running her fingers through her hair distractedly.

"Well, you are going to have them whether you want them or not, and fairly soon by the look of things," the vet said.

"Not today or tomorrow though?" asked Matt's mother, her face horrified.

"No, not as soon as that. In about two weeks' time," said the vet. "Try to get her to walk a little. We want to get rid of the congestion on her chest."

"What about her swollen leg? Shouldn't we bathe it?" asked Matt.

"No, the penicillin will take care of that. But you were only just in time. Another day and she wouldn't have been with us. Where are you going next?" he asked, snapping his case shut.

"We don't know yet. We can't take Jessie to a hotel in her condition," replied Matt's mother. "We're at our wits' end."

It was then that Matt remembered Anne's letter. It was still in the pocket of his jeans. He pulled it out and looked at the address: Frognal, Hampstead.

"We can go to Hampstead, Mum. It *is* in London, isn't it?" he cried. "We can stay with Anne's granny. Anne's invited me. Look, it's all here in this letter," he continued, waving the letter and laughing at his mother's perplexed face. "We can take a taxi, no problem."

"Sounds an excellent solution," commented the vet,

133

accepting a croissant from Linda.

"I know they'll have Jessie," Matt cried . . . And Jessie, hearing her name mentioned and the happiness in Matt's voice, wagged her tail; then sat up smiling at Matt with her eyes. It was a smile which said everything: "I'm content. I love you. Everything is going to be all right because we're together again."

Thirteen

THEY promised to ring the vet when they were settled and he departed, smiling in between munches at a second croissant. Then Matt telephoned Anne, shrieking over the telephone. "It's me—Matt. We're in London."

"London! But I thought you were in Florida," she shrieked back, and suddenly the room was electric with excitement.

"We've got Jessie. She's ill. It's a long, long story. Can we come and stay, just for a night or two?" asked Matt.

"You and Jessie?"

"Yes, and Mum for a night, just to get straight. Is that possible?"

"I'll just ask Gran."

"Anne did ask me. I've got the letter to prove it," said Matt, smiling at his mother.

"Yes, we've seen it. You waved it over our heads just a minute ago," she reminded him.

"Yes, fine. Gran says she's delighted. She says, shall she get some dog food in?" asked Anne, laughing.

"No, it's all right. Jessie isn't eating yet. She's been very ill. On a drip. It's been awful. We'll be coming by taxi. Will half an hour be too soon?" asked Matt.

"It will take you longer than that, but of course it is all right. Come as soon as you can."

His mother was already packing, throwing things into their two small cases anyhow, not caring, just glad to have somewhere to go.

"I've lost all sense of time, and it's so lovely to have Jessie again. I just can't believe it, but she is ill, really ill," Matt shrieked down the telephone.

"I'm so sorry. Poor Jess! Take care. See you soon," Anne said.

"Bye." Matt put down the receiver as his mother asked, "It's really all right? I'll ring for a taxi, then."

They gave Denise and Linda the wine and chocolates, and money to cover the telephone calls they had made. "I don't know how to thank you," said Matt's mother.

"It was nothing, absolutely nothing," Denise answered.

"We would do it again any time. I hope Jessie recovers," Linda added, smiling.

"We'll let you know," Matt told them, his face creased into a smile, all the sorrow gone from it, only happiness shining out and infecting all of them.

"I rang Dad last night. I didn't tell you because you were asleep," his mother said, putting on her coat. "He says to spare no expense to get Jessie well again, and he sends you his love."

"That's all right, then," said Matt, collecting Jessie's toys. He put them in her basket, thinking how it seemed a lifetime since he had done exactly the same thing. Jessie watched him anxiously. The doorbell rang. Matt and his mother carried Jessie still wrapped in a blanket down the stairs, while Denise followed carrying the basket with Jessie's toys inside. Matt kept one hand on Jessie's anxious face all the time, saying, "It's all right, not to worry. We'll never desert you again."

Smiling, a ferret-faced taxi driver held the door of his cab open for them. Another minute and they were on their way, not talking, just watching Jessie. Matt was thinking what a miracle it was that they had found her in time, and his mother that Matt would never give her up now. She had never realized he had it in him to love anything as much. Jessie watched them both, but chiefly Matt. It would be a long time before she would trust anyone again, but already the ordeals of the last months were beginning to fade from her mind. Even Eric mattered less now that she had Matt.

"We must ring the hospital and send a message to Eric. Why didn't I think of it before?" cried Matt's mother as they neared Hampstead. "He'll be so pleased to hear we've found Jessie."

Matt smiled. He hardly wanted to talk any more now that he had Jessie. If only she could talk, he thought—there's so much I would like to know. Jessie was licking her injured paw now. Her eyes were almost clear, her breath coming more easily. "Thank God for penicillin," exclaimed Matt's mother, watching her. "She's going to be all right and we're going to have some pups: you realize that, don't you, Matt?"

He nodded, unable to speak for fear of breaking the spell which seemed to hang over them at that moment . . . a strange mixture of relief, hope and happiness.

Anne threw open an old-fashioned front door. "Come in, come in," she cried. "Oh, poor Jessie!"

Matt was relieved to find Anne had not changed, was just the same, same old smile, same hair, same everything.

"I fear we are a terrible invasion," his mother said to Anne's grandmother. "It is so good of you to have us."

Later when they had talked and talked and eaten a hearty meal, while Jessie lay comfortably in her basket watching Matt with adoring eyes, they opened Eric's mail. There was quite a pile of it—Matt's letter, which had taken an age to reach London because of a postman's strike, his postcard from New York, a heap of bills in red.

Also there were two official-looking letters. Matt's mother read the first of these slowly before crying. "Oh, would you believe it? Eric's won an award and should have gone to Stationers' Hall in October to receive it!" Then, tearing the other envelope open, she cried, "And here's a check for three thousand pounds, and all for those darned old scarecrows. Oh, I am so pleased. It's second prize for the Inventor of the Year! Good old Eric. And we always laughed at him. What a turnaround!"

"Let me look," cried Matt, leaping to his feet, while Anne said, "I thought you said he was looney."

"And here's a letter from a businessman who wants to develop the scarecrows on a commerical basis, who thinks they should be exported to the Third World.

Eric's going to be rich at last. Oh, I'm so pleased," cried his mother, jumping up and down. "It looks as though a farmer in Kent entered one of the scarecrows on Eric's behalf. Was sorry for him, I expect. You wait till I tell your father, Matt. It feels like Christmas already, doesn't it? I must go and see Eric first thing. I'll stay near the hospital for a few days and help him get better."

Matt had never seen his mother so excited before. "I always knew he was different from other people," he said.

"I think this calls for a toast," suggested Anne's granny, who looked too young to be a granny, who wore jeans and training shoes and an oiled fisherman's sweater, and kept a dog of her own called Kim, a hairy little cross bred dog from Battersea Dogs' Home.

"We'll toast to Jessie and Eric," said Matt.

"Can Matt stay with you for another day or two while I nurse Eric? And I must find us a house to rent over Christmas, before we settle in East Anglia," said Matt's mother when they were sitting calmly round the gas fire in the sitting room, recovering from so much good news. "It seems an awful lot to ask."

"Of course. It will be lovely, won't it, Anne?" said her granny, smiling. "We're very dull on our own. And when Jessie's better she can walk on the heath with Kim."

And now Matt was imagining Eric sitting up in his hospital bed, listening to Matt's mother as she told him the good news, his face lighting up to hear he need never be poor again.

"I would like to meet a real inventor. Can you bring back his autograph, Mrs. Painter?" Anne asked.

"When he can write I'll get one for you," replied Matt's mother.

"I just can't believe that Jessie is going to be all right. It's like a miracle, isn't it?" Matt said.

"And soon you will have lots of little Jessies," said Anne, laughing. "I wonder what they will be like. I wonder what their father was."

"All right, because Jessie would not mate with any old dog: you can be sure of that," answered Matt. "You can have one of them if you like, Anne—you and your granny, because you're the best friends we'll ever have. You can have the pick of the litter."

"You must come and stay with us when we find a house—both of you. My husband has asked for a transfer to Holland. That way he can commute from Norwich by air and Matt need never change schools again. We are going to buy a house with plenty of room for lots of people, with outbuildings and an orchard—a real home at last," said Matt's mother, laughing.

"We'll have James to stay too, because he never has a proper holiday," Matt said.

And now he could see it all—an old house dreaming amid trees, a barn, and acres of garden where Jessie could dig holes and bury bones, where she could roam at will, along with her pups still to be born. A real home with room for Eric to stay while he recovered. A place they could call their own. A home for Jessie.

About the Author

CHRISTINE PULLEIN-THOMPSON has written
children's stories for over 40 years. Born in Surrey,
England, in 1930, she writes about animals surviving
in the wild, raising ponies in the countryside, and
hunting with woodland foxhounds.

At about age 15, Pullein-Thompson wrote her first
book with her two sisters. Most of her stories have
been about ponies.

Now she is director of a riding school. When she
finds time, she writes children's books from her home
in Suffolk, England, where she lives with her family,
ponies, cats, dogs, and hens.